Praise

"The author's capacity f [barcode: D0462146] ters vividly to life is envial _____ age novelist."—*New York Times Book Review*

"Sidhwa is a superb storyteller."—*New Internationalist*

"Bapsi Sidhwa is a writer of enormous talent, capable of endowing small domestic occurrences with cosmic drama and rendering calamitous historical events with deeply felt personal meaning."—*New York Newsday*

"A powerful and dramatic novelist."—*The Times*

"An affectionate and shrewd observer...a born storyteller." —*The New Statesman*

"Sidhwa is a rarity even in swiftly changing Asia—a candid, forthright, balanced woman novelist. Her twentieth-century view of Indian life can only be compared to V.S. Naipaul's. Sidhwa is among the most invigorating Indian writers." —*Bloomsbury Review*

"Sidhwa writes dramatically of marriage, loyalty, honour and their conflict with old ways."—*Publisher's Weekly*

"There is a Kiplingesque quality to Sidhwa's writing, the congenital ability to make one feel the ambiance of the locale." —*Houston Chronicle*

"Bapsi Sidhwa writes with immense vigour and liveliness." —*Good Housekeeping*

Also by the Author
An American Brat
Cracking India
The Bride
The Crow Eaters

WATER

A Novel Based on the Film by Deepa Mehta

Bapsi Sidhwa

KEY PORTER BOOKS

Copyright © 2006 by Bapsi Sidhwa

Based on the film script for *Water* by Deepa Mehta

All rights reserved. No part of this work covered by the copyrights hereon may be reproduced or used in any form or by any means—graphic, electronic or mechanical, including photocopying, recording, taping or information storage and retrieval systems—without the prior written permission of the publisher, or, in case of photocopying or other reprographic copying, a licence from Access Copyright, the Canadian Copyright Licensing Agency, One Yonge Street, Suite 1900, Toronto, Ontario, M6B 3A9.

Library and Archives Canada Cataloguing in Publication

Sidhwa, Bapsi
    Water : a novel based on the film by Deepa Mehta / Bapsi Sidhwa.

ISBN 1-55263-753-0

    I. Title.

PR9540.9.S53W37   2006   823'.914   C2005-906158-8

The publisher gratefully acknowledges the support of the Canada Council for the Arts and the Ontario Arts Council for its publishing program. We acknowledge the support of the Government of Ontario through the Ontario Media Development Corporation's Ontario Book Initiative.

We acknowledge the financial support of the Government of Canada through the Book Publishing Industry Development Program (BPIDP) for our publishing activities.

Key Porter Books Limited
Six Adelaide Street East, Tenth Floor
Toronto, Ontario
Canada M5C 1H6

www.keyporter.com

Text design: Marijke Friesen
Electronic formatting: Jean Lightfoot Peters

Printed and bound in Canada

06 07 08 09 10 5 4 3

For Deepa Mehta

*And for Mohur, Parizad and Baku,
the other beloved women in my life*

Prologue

1936
Setting: A village on the Bihar–Bengal border

All at once, Chuyia tired of playing with her clay dolls. Her mouth craved something sweet. She knew exactly where she would find some ripe gooseberries. She packed up her toys and pushed the box against the wall of the neglected thatched hut that lay at the far corner of their compound. The forest that came right up to the edge of their wall had claimed the hut with swathes of china-rose and a tangle of thick-stalked creepers.

Chuyia squeezed through a hedge of castor-oil trees and skipped along a path in her bare feet. A couple of days back, she had discovered the gooseberry bushes just off the narrow path that ran through some mango and jackfruit orchards and led into the jungle. She had walked a long way into the forest with her brothers but had never come to its end. The path held drooping clusters of fruit on the tamarind trees, and, once, she had come upon a clump of wild leechee trees. Chuyia soon found the gooseberry bushes and, after savouring the fruit's tart sweetness, began collecting the berries in her skirt for her mother to pickle. But this proved cumbersome, so Chuyia ate the gooseberries instead.

Chuyia had wandered deep into the forest in search of wild leechees when she became aware of the distant whining and whimpering of an animal; it was in distress. Abandoning her search for leechees, she made her way through the undergrowth, which was for the most part taller than she was. Although it was midday, the rays of the sun barely penetrated the thick green canopy that formed a roof over her head.

Every now and then Chuyia stopped to listen to make sure she was heading toward the source of the cries. She had little fear of the forest, and was as familiar with it as a child brought up near the ocean is familiar with its shores.

As she drew closer to the sound, she became puzzled. Muffled by the dense vegetation, the yelping and mewling seemed to surround her—and yet she couldn't locate the terrified creature. Chuyia pushed back branches and crouched to search through the thicket of plants mouldering underneath for want of sunlight. She thrashed through the young bamboo saplings and skirted the ancient drooping clumps.

Chuyia came upon a small clearing and, after parting the foliage and pushing back the creepers that concealed the ditch, she discovered a scruffy little pup that had fallen through. Barely distinguishable from the bed of decaying leaves, it was feebly trying to scramble up the steep sides of the ditch and slipping back.

"Tun-tun, Tun-tun," Chuyia called softly.

Tun-tun was the generic name given by the village children to all the local mongrels that prowled the neighbourhood and from time to time attached themselves to the houses that fed them scraps. With their short, dun-coloured fur and straight-up tails, they were almost indistinguishable from one another, except for the grov-elling bitches with swinging teats who slunk around with their tails between their legs.

The puppy cocked its pointy ears to look at her and increased the volume of its yelping. Holding on to a sup-ple young bamboo, Chuyia lowered herself down the incline. The startled pup growled and backed away from the alarming proximity to the stranger. It bared its tiny teeth. Chuyia noticed the small protrusion low down its belly and decided it was a boy. She squatted at the base of the ditch and remained still to give the nervous animal time to get accustomed to her. She wanted Tun-tun to know she wouldn't harm him, and was prepared to get acquainted with him on his terms.

After a while, she edged closer and held out her hand. "Tun-tun, Tun-tun," she said softly, making gentle kiss-ing sounds. "Come to me. Come," she cajoled.

His tail wagging tentatively, the animal cocked its head to look at her but held its ground.

Wary of the sharp little teeth, Chuyia slowly reached out to touch its grubby head. At her touch, Tun-tun rolled over on his back and, his little tail thumping the dirt, twisted his body this way and that, as if posing for the cutest effect. Still squatting, Chuyia waddled closer and gingerly stroked his belly. The dog's little tail thumped harder. What an adorable face he had. She tried again to stroke his head and the pup quickly licked her fingers with his wet tongue. Chuyia retracted her hand reflexively.

Bit by bit, each sized up the other.

Chuyia felt an overwhelming surge of tenderness and longing and, reaching out with both hands, picked up the pup. She did it so clumsily that the discomfited creature wiggled free and fell to the ground. She hunkered down on her heels, and the puppy began to sniff at her dusty feet. All at once, it braced its tiny paws against her knees and licked her face. Chuyia laughed. She cradled the little fellow in her arms and allowed him to lick her neck. Stroking and kissing the puppy, covering him with the flap of her blouse to protect him from the prickly twigs, she carried Tun-tun through the forest.

Chapter One

Bhagya sat cross-legged on the kitchen floor, grinding rice with a mortar and pestle and adding it to the flour she stored in a brass jar. Dusk had thickened into night outside the kitchen window, and the hectic twittering of the birds had given way to the muted sounds of nocturnal animals of the forest and the sudden orchestration of cicadas. Her day's chores done, her family fed, this was Bhagya's hour of solitude. The rhythmic pounding of the pestle and her automated movements had a meditative quality, and she often chanted or hummed holy passages from the Bhagvad Gita or the Mahabharata at this time.

Somnath came into the kitchen with the box of betel nut and, after adjusting his crumpled night *dhoti*, quietly squatted beneath the pots lined up on a shelf nailed to the wall. Although Bhagya had her back to him, she was aware of his presence. She brought her sari forward to cover her bare shoulder and head. Somnath waited patiently. Even though her body had thickened with child-bearing, she was as beautiful as the Goddess Bhagyalakshmi, whose name she bore. And with the passion of youth diluted by the daily grind of household tasks and the passage of time, she was surely as pure as the Goddess Sita.

Bhagya wondered what had brought her husband to the kitchen. He usually left her alone to finish her chores. She sensed it had something to do with his visit to the widower Hira Lal's house earlier that morning. On his return from the house, he had barely spoken to her or to the children. Hira Lal's mother had sent for him, and Bhagya had assumed it had to do with the prayer rituals Somnath often performed at their house. Now she wondered what it was; she would find out soon enough.

Bhagya added the last lot of ground rice to the jar and pushed the pestle and mortar against the wall. She placed the lid on the jar and turned her head slightly.

"You wish to say something?"

Somnath patted the clean clay floor. "Come, sit by me."

Bhagya wiped her hands on her sari and sat down cross-legged where he had indicated. She pulled the box to her and started spreading the red *katha* paste on the betel leaf. She glanced at him. "What's the matter?"

"Why should anything be the matter?" Somnath said. "Don't look so serious, I bring you good news."

Bhagya searched his face from the corner of her eyes. Although he was trying to smile, the drawn lines on his face belied his words. Something was the matter.

"So, tell me," she said.

Holding his hand out to receive the betel leaf, Somnath breathed out in a way that was almost a sigh. "Hira Lal's mother wants our Chuyia to marry Hira Lal," he said.

Bhagya lifted the edge of her sari and lowered her head to disguise the sudden tumult that agitated her heart and left her short of breath. She waited for him to continue.

"I have agreed," he said. "Their horoscopes match. We have looked at some auspicious dates. They want the marriage to take place before Diwali—in September or October. The monsoon will be over and our guests can sleep outside."

"She is only six," Bhagya said, her quavering voice so low Somnath had to strain to catch her words. "I've heard Hira Lal is a grandfather."

"He's younger than me, about forty-four," Somnath said. "They don't want a dowry; they will pay for the wedding. She will be well cared for. Hira Lal's mother is a kind woman. She will be good to our girl."

"Shouldn't you have consulted me?" said Bhagya.

Somnath stretched his legs out and, adjusting the fall of the sacred thread that ran diagonally across his bare chest, leaned back. Although the flesh on his chest was spare, his stomach protruded in a small, spongy roll. He swallowed the juice that had collected in his mouth and, tucking the betel into one cheek, said, "How could I refuse Hira Lal's mother?"

Bhagya drew her sari forward so that her face was in shadow. "It is settled then! Why bother to tell me? So what if I have never set eyes on the man?" She had not spoken to him so harshly in a long while.

"He's not bad-looking. The family is of noble Brahmin lineage. We should be honoured," Somnath said, and, in an attempt to placate her, he added, "Our

13

little mouse will remain with us until she comes of age. She will play with her friends, have a normal childhood."

"*Ishh*, Bhagwan: may she never come of age!" Bhagya spat out the words.

"Don't speak such ill-omened words," he said uneasily, shaking his head reprovingly. "A girl is destined to leave her parents' home early or she will bring disgrace to it. She is safe and happy only in her husband's care."

"She is safe and happy enough in our care."

"In the Brahmanical tradition," said Somnath, shifting into the soothing and at the same time authoritative mode he adopted when speaking to his clients, "a woman is recognized as a person only when she is one with her husband. Only then does she become a *sumangali*, an auspicious woman, and a *saubhagyavati*, a fortunate woman." And, as if recalling a passage from a holy book, he half-closed his lids to add, "A woman's body is a site for conflict between a demonic *stri-svavahava*, which is her lustful aspect, and her *stri-dharma*, which is her womanly duty."

Bhagya jerked her head up so that her sari fell from her hair and stared at him. "And you think that man will be able to satisfy her *stri-svavahava*? By the time her womanhood blooms, he'll be old and spent."

Somnath was shocked. Although he well knew his wife's passionate nature and discreetly relished it, her lust was contained within the parameters sanctioned by marriage. But to hear her speak so crudely about his daughter's sexuality violated the principles upon which his ideas of sanctity were based. The Brahmin elders were right: women were dangerous. They sapped a man's strength and stood between him and salvation. He leaned forward to stare at the woman confronting him.

The hard glint in her husband's eyes pierced Bhagya like an arrow hurled by the God Arjuna; he had never looked at her this way before. Frozen with the weight of a hoary tradition that brooked no deviation, his look chilled her blood.

"You are the wife and daughter of Brahmin priests; surely you are aware of our traditions," he said. "Outside of marriage the wife has no recognized existence in our tradition. A woman's role in life is to get married and have sons. That is why she is created: to have sons! That is all!"

Bhagya, overwhelmed by her husband's fury, knew she had overstepped her bounds. She dropped her eyes. Her husband was right; his words bore the cumulative wisdom of gods and ancient sages, and who was she to challenge that august pantheon? A girl carried within her the seeds of dishonour, and the burden of responsibility was to be borne by her parents until she was married. "I am sorry," she said humbly, duly chastened. "It's just that I hadn't thought about her marriage. She scampers all about the place like her namesake, Little Mouse. I need time to get used to the idea of her absence from our house. It will be as you say—you are her father."

Bhagya carried the kitchen lamp into the children's bedroom. Her sons Prasad and Mohan were asleep on the thin mattress on their hard bed. She sat down on the edge of Chuyia's cot and held the earthenware lamp so that its light bathed her daughter's face in a coppery glow. Her curling eyelashes cast shadows on her cheeks, and her face was full and round like the moon that had arisen and now shone through the window. Her mouth was an inlaid bud in the moon of her face. Impulsively, she bent to lightly kiss the sweetness on her daughter's lips. The wash-worn rag that served as Chuyia's tiny sari had ridden up her thighs, and, with her sturdy, rounded limbs, she looked like one of Krishna's cherubic *gopis*.

Bhagya was not given to looking at her daughter so closely. She often gazed upon her sons as they slept. She covertly observed them when they were absorbed in school work or having the extra portion of food she had saved for them, and then her heart brimmed over with love and the special pride that was her due as mother of sons. She fretted about them because they were pale, and their thin limbs and stalk-like necks gave them an appearance of fragility. Bhagya never worried about her robust daughter and, scolding her for her playful and wilful ways, plied her sturdy little body with work—fetch the water, carry the firewood, sweep the yard, feed the cow.

Bhagya pried loose a strand of hair from Chuyia's neck, and with her sari patted dry the moisture that had formed in the crease where her neck joined her collarbone. Chuyia's hair, which already fell to her waist, spread about her in a velvet tangle of curls. Bhagya knew she must have looked like this at Chuyia's age. Then why did she not lavish on her the affection and attention she lavished on her sons? Feel the same surge of love and pride for her daughter? Was it because her heart knew that a daughter was only a guest and never belonged to the house into which she was born? As she looked down at her daughter's baby face, Bhagya's eyes became moist and she was swept by a wave of tenderness and pity she had not allowed herself to feel before. She kissed her daughter's forehead and brushed her eyelids with her lips.

All at once the girl opened huge eyes, and in the lamplight they appeared clear and luminous with understanding, as if the child had grasped the complexity and paradox of her mother's emotions. Bhagya stroked her daughter's cheeks. She whispered, "Go to sleep, my little mouse." The girl's heavy lids slowly sheathed her eyes and, as if the taut skin of her eyelids were insufficient to cover them, left milky crescents beneath her eyelashes. Flesh of my flesh, the beautiful fruit of my womb: her gaze lingered on her daughter's face.

Bhagya sat up, suddenly filled with a guilty sense of foreboding; a mother's unbridled love would surely attract *nazar* to her child. Bhagya snapped her fingers thrice in quick succession to ward off the evil eye. She drew her sari over her bowed head and, folding her hands, prayed to Shashthi, the goddess of children, to watch over her sleeping daughter.

≫≪

BHAGYA HAD RECITED HER morning prayers by the time the boys left for school. As she watered the holy basil bushes, Somnath, in white *dhoti* and shirt, armed with his basket of sacred texts and the caste-marks on his forehead, came looking for her.

"*Accha*, I'm going," he said by way of farewell.

Bhagya covered her head. "Bring plantain. If you can, some fish for the children."

Somnath nodded confidently. "I'm owed quite a bit."

"Our neighbour said a holy man has come from far away. His name is Gandhi. Get his picture if you can for my prayer nook."

"Yes, people are talking about him; they call him *bapu* Gandhi," Somnath said. "He wants us to weave our own cloth—the English *sarkar* thinks he is a trouble-maker—but I hear he is a good man. He says all religions are true. He wants people to unite in their struggle against the English's *raj*. I'll look for his picture in the bazaar." And then Somnath set off for far-flung houses to collect the meagre tithes that were his due as a Brahmin.

Chuyia helped her mother pick up her brothers' soiled clothes for the wash and rolled up the bedding. She went to the back of the house to lay out the feed and fill the water bucket for the cow and its wobbly-legged calf. When she returned, she found her mother reclining by the window and chanting from the Mahabharata. Bhagya often did this before preparing her midday meal. Chuyia promptly covered her head with her sari and snuggled up to her mother, intent on listening to the passionate stories of the gods and goddesses. Bhagya arranged her sari to accommodate Chuyia and began to read out from the tattered copy of the Mahabharata.

A covey of parrots, the sudden whir from their wings startling them, streaked greenly past their window on the way to the neighbour's orchard. Chuyia didn't mind sharing the fruit with the parrots: in any case, they would forage among the higher branches she couldn't reach.

After the sacred text had been put away, Chuyia followed her mother into the kitchen. She prattled away about the doings of the deities as Bhagya, sitting on the palm leaf mat on the floor, sliced onions and prepared the spinach. Bhagya answered her questions distractedly. Chuyia watched her mother rinse the spinach. "Why don't you cook fish? I'm tired of spinach," she said. "Radha's ma cooks fish every day."

"If your father brings it, I'll cook it," she said. "You'll get as much fish as you want at your husband's house."

Chuyia slipped her sari off her little shoulder and spread it between her hands. "I want this much!"

Her daughter's chest was flat and her small nipples dimpled inwards. Bhagya had an urge to hold her. She cleaned her fingers and reaching forward, swung the child to her lap. "Don't worry; he'll fill your lap with mangoes and almond taffy," she said. "But will you share it with him," she teased, "or will you gobble it all up yourself?"

Chuyia, dazzled by the unsustainable images of abundance her mother conjured up, nodded shyly and buried her face in Bhagya's soft bosom.

Bhagya got up when the mustard oil in the *karahi* began to smoke. She dropped a pinch of salt and turmeric into the oil and stirred the onions into it.

"Let me do that," Chuyia said.

"No, you'll burn yourself."

"But I want to help you cook," Chuyia importuned. "I want to help you."

To keep her daughter away from the wok, Bhagya gave her a steel platter half-filled with lentils. "Here; remove the grit and small stones from the *daal* if you must help."

But this didn't conform with Chuyia's idea of cooking. After a short while, she announced, "*Amma*, I've cleaned the *daal*," and put the steel platter aside.

Bhagya looked up from the potatoes she was peeling. "Either you put your heart into what you're doing, or you don't do it at all."

"Then don't tell me to clean *daal*. I can't put my heart into lentils!"

"*Hai*, what a rude girl you've become," said Bhagya, taken aback. Not for the first time she thought, the child is old for her years. "If you talk back to your mother-in-law like this, she will shame me for not bringing you up properly," she said aloud, dramatically smacking her head to convey the humiliation that lay in store for her.

"I'll tell her, 'Don't shame my mother,'" said Chuyia heartlessly. She climbed on a stool and reached for the clay pot of *mishti-doi* that Bhagya had made with rich milk from their cow, which had just calved. "It's empty," she wailed.

"There was only a little left. Your brothers must have eaten it."

"*Amma*, I want *mishti-doi*. Please make some, please, please," whined Chuyia.

Bhagya flung an arm out and thwacked Chuyia, catching her on her thigh. "Go play outside before I lose my temper and thrash you."

Chuyia stepped out of her mother's reach and, holding her hands behind her back, obdurately shook her head. "There is no one to play with."

Bhagya made a small cone with a scrap of paper and got up to fill it with roasted gram. "Here, feed your dolls this," she said, pushing Chuyia out the door.

Chuyia called Tun-tun, but he wasn't around. Munching on the roasted chickpeas, Chuyia crossed their yard to the thatched hut. A tangle of mossy branches weighed down the roof, and the small yard in front was overgrown with weeds. Chuyia pried open the door that hung crookedly from its hinges. It was dark inside the hut, and the cooler air held the sweet odours of damp earth and vegetation that had taken root in the earth floor.

Chuyia dragged the doll's house, a rough plywood crate the size of two shoeboxes, to the centre of the room and, in the light that came from a sagging slit of skylight, examined its contents. She picked up the chipped clay dolls, the faded outlines of their stiff, glazed arms barely discernable against their torsos, and wiped them with her sari. She talked to her dolls as she tipped the contents of her toy box and lined up the miniature cooking utensils in front of a brick, which served as a make-believe stove. "You must be hungry; I'll cook you turnips," she told the dolls, pulling out some spongy weeds growing through the cracks of the floor. She squished them and collected the pulp in a tiny *karahi*. She added the few remaining chickpeas from the paper cone to the mess and stirred it with a minuscule ladle.

Chuyia force-fed her dolls with the food she had prepared and, when the green slime stained their faces, scolded them for being dirty. She used the same words and tone of voice Bhagya used, except she kept her voice hushed, lest someone should intrude on her imagined world and break the spell of make-believe she had conjured up.

Tun-tun's shrill little barks returned her to reality and filled her heart with love. Although he sounded less puppyish now, his voice still broke at the higher octaves. Abandoning her dolls Chuyia went outside to greet the now-brawny little fellow. Before long, they both wandered off into the jungle.

Tun-tun kept within calling distance as Chuyia foraged for wild berries and leechees. After a while, she lay down on a bed of yellow leaves fallen from a thorn tree, and Tun-tun, placing his forelegs on her chest, pinned her down and gazed at her for all the world like a conquering lion. He licked her face. Chuyia pushed him away, and, after chasing a squirrel up a tree, he settled down beside her to keep watch.

High above, the thorn tree was in blossom, and the fragrance from its flowers mingled with the other windborne scents of the forest. A tailor bird was stitching its nest in the fork of a dried branch, and, at a small distance from her, a pair of canaries sat swinging on creepers that hung down from a jackfruit tree. Birds hopped among the branches of trees, making the leaves tremble and filling the forest with birdsong. The squirrels played hide-and-seek around tree trunks. Closer to the ground, her ears picked up the rustle of fecund vegetation and of unseen insects inhabiting it. All of Chuyia's senses became steeped in the forest's wild beauty—her pulse slowed to match its deep green rhythm, and her heart was at peace.

Chapter Two

≈

A flurry of activity overtook their household. Huge colanders of rice and lentils simmered on wood fires in the backyard. Small boxes filled with sweet *laddoos*, and smeared with turmeric and red *kum-kum* to mark the auspicious nature of the occasion, were sent to neighbours. Marquees were set up, palm leaf mats spread on the ground, and the guests were served food on washed banana leaves.

Mohan and Prasad were packed off to a neighbour's house. Chuyia slept with Bhagya.

The day before the wedding, women gathered around the sweet tulsi bushes in their yard to sing songs. Chuyia was excited by all the activity centred on her, but some of the more doleful songs about the bride's sorrow at leaving her parents' house made her anxious. "I don't want to leave you and *baba*," she cried, clinging to Bhagya's sari. "I don't want to leave Mohan *bhaiya* and Prasad *bhaiya* or Tun-tun. I will have no one to play with," she said, weeping bitterly.

This behaviour was not only expected of her, it was considered commendable.

Some of the women, remembering their own weddings, shed copious tears, saying, "*Hai*, poor little thing. It is never easy to leave your parents' house. She has no idea of the troubles that lie ahead for her."

Hearing them, Chuyia howled louder and clung closer to her mother. When this had gone on for some time and the women were suitably impressed, Bhagya took her hysterical and bewildered daughter to one side. Wiping her tears, she said, "Don't worry. You won't go to your husband's house for a long, long time. You can play with your brothers all you want until then."

"Can I take my brothers with me?" Chuyia asked.

Bhagya smiled. "No, you can't take them."

"Can I take Tun-tun?"

Bhagya pretended to mull over the question. "Okay. We will give him to you as part of your dowry," she said. "We will also give you the cow so that you will have plenty of milk and *mishti-doi* in your husband's house."

⫘

THE DAY OF THE WEDDING BEGAN early for the bride with the Haldi Uptan ritual. Chuyia's aunt rubbed the turmeric paste all over her niece's firm little body. Chuyia looked down at her body askance. "I don't want to turn yellow," she cried, trying to wiggle out of her aunt's grasp. "My friends will laugh at me. Wash it off!"

"You won't turn yellow. You'll turn golden, and your husband will be dazzled by your beauty."

"I don't want a husband!" Chuyia said petulantly. "I don't want to get married."

"Marriage and death are not in our hands. They are in Bhagwan's hands," her aunt said firmly. Then she laughed. "Don't worry; the *uptan* has magical properties that will make you love your husband." She looked at the naked, asexual little creature standing disconsolately in front of her, and her expression softened. "You don't understand what I'm saying, do you? You will in a few years—when our mouse is ready to go to her husband's house." And before Chuyia could speak, she added, "You will understand a lot of things then—so shush now."

After the beauty treatment, seven married women—relatives and favoured neighbours—in turn squeezed Chuyia's supple hands in theirs to push tight red-and-green glass marriage bangles onto her wrists. Chuyia bore the ordeal happily and shook her arms to show off the jingling bangles to her envious friends. The seven women represented the seven forms of God, one for each day of the week. Since their village was situated on the Bengal–Bihar border, the rituals represented a mixture of Hindu customs from both provinces.

Chuyia was shown the presents the groom had sent her—jewellery, which included a gold *mangal-sutra* necklace, and several saris for her to change into on the wedding day. Elaborate makeup was applied to her face, with small white dots over the eyebrows, and her hair was decorated with flowers and stuck with the ornaments she asked for: sun, moon, stars made of tinsel. A gold chain was placed along the part in her hair and another around her neck.

The wedding took place in the village temple. Preparations were underway to feed the guests, and the entire village would receive a helping of sweet rice and milk *kheer* served in shallow earthenware dishes. Since the presence of menstruating women would defile the wedding and pollute the temple, food would be left for them at their doors.

Children ran around shouting and playing in the large compound, but the main attraction was the temple elephant and its year-old baby. They watched, enchanted, as the *pujari* fed the wrinkle-hided little elephant bananas. Later on, they would get to ride in the *howda* already strapped on to the big elephant's back.

As the bride, borne in a palanquin, and the groom in elaborate head-gear (both preceded by ragged village bands) made their separate way to the wedding hall, the women from villages in Bengal ululated to draw attention to the wedding ceremony itself; a conch was blown to complement the "*oolu-oolu,*" in keeping with the tradition.

An admiring murmur rose among the onlookers, and Bhagya turned her head to gaze upon her son-in-law as he entered the temple. Hira Lal carried his forty-four years lightly, and he appeared to support the decorated cake-like headgear—rising almost a foot above his head—with ease. He looked at least a decade younger than Somnath. "Not bad-looking," Somnath had said. With the deep cleft in his chin and the glow of health suffusing his features, yes, Hira Lal was not bad-looking.

Only Brahmins were allowed inside the temple. Since the temple hall had no walls—just the tall pillars that supported the roof—everyone could see the wedding ceremony as it took place. The guests nodded their heads and made approving sounds as Somnath presented Hira Lal with a gold ring, a new *dhoti* and a handsome new umbrella. It was a ritual they were familiar with and enjoyed.

Bhagya thought of her sons and wondered, would she be able to give them the quantity of milk and fat and fish that had nourished Hira Lal's trim body? And even as she mutely appealed to Lakshmi, the goddess of wealth, to bless her household, her misgivings concerning her daughter's betrothed quieted. The goddess had favoured her, but she had been too thick-headed to recognize it; it was plain to see that the connection with Hira Lal's family would benefit her household.

Chuyia was made to sit in front of *Agni*, the sacred fire. The sari, pulled over her face, narrowed her vision like blinders.

Bhagya could barely recognize her daughter; seated next to the groom, she looked like a diminutive doll. Hira Lal sat cross-legged within the graceful folds of his white *dhoti*, the sacred thread prominent across his bare chest. A corner of Chuyia's sari was tied to a long stole wrapped around Hira Lal's neck and shoulders, and they were made to stand. With *Agni*, the Holy Fire as witness, the groom and his bride walked seven times around a pattern on the floor. Bhagya hid her smile in her sari; Hira Lal appeared linked to the ambulatory little bundle in red silk as to a pet. The *purohit* reverentially fed *Agni* with rarified butter and frankincense and, chanting mantras to invoke the blessings of the gods, solemnized the marriage.

Hira Lal's eldest sister brought the traditional *Sindoor Daan* on a tray. The groom applied the red *sindoor* to the parting in the bride's hair and to her forehead. As a Hindu woman, the bride would wear this symbol from the time of the *Sindoor Daan* until her death. Of all the ceremonial gifts, the *kanya daan*, or bride-gift, is considered to be the holiest. Just as the giver can no longer lay claim to an object that has once been donated, the parents of a traditional Hindu bride have no rights over their daughter once she has been gifted to the bridegroom. The groom then offered his bride a new sari with which to cover her head, and with this act the couple was considered officially married.

Chapter Three

As the demand for her husband's service grew, Bhagya expended a small fortune on joss sticks and sandalwood and spent more time praying to the pantheon of gods and goddesses ensconced between her cupboards. Twice a day, drenched in gratitude, she prostrated herself before the Goddess Lakshmi and, weaving jasmine garlands from the bushes in her compound, hung them around the goddess's neck.

"Once the goddess decides to give, she is not stingy," Somnath declared between mouthfuls of a fiery fish curry mixed with rice, as Bhagya fanned him with a palm leaf. "She tears asunder the sky to let wealth pour through in a multitude of forms."

Bhagya nodded in agreement, as she spooned more rice into Somnath's plate and poured more curry into the hole he made in the rice with his fingers. She had just told him that their cow had calved and, because of the improved quality of its feed, was giving richer after-birth milk than ever before.

Except for an occasional reprimand in the months following the marriage, there was no marked difference in Chuyia's carefree life. When Bhagya remembered to, she would say, "Cover your head, you're a married woman now," or, "You mustn't go jumping in the pond and wandering off into the forest like this: if your mother-in-law finds out she won't like it." Chuyia would do as she was told for a few days and then return to her old ways until her mother remembered to scold her again.

She continued to play with her brothers, romp around with the other village children, and wander off into the forest at will.

By the end of two years, Chuyia had almost no memory of her wedding.

⧼

WHEN SOMNATH HAD FIRST come home with the news that Hira Lal was ill, neither Bhagya nor he thought it was anything to worry about. People got sick, and after a while they recovered. And Hira Lal was a strapping fellow, glowing with health.

However, five days later, Bhagya guessed from the sombre look on Somnath's face, as he came into the kitchen and sat down on the mat, that things were not going well with Hira Lal: what else would cause him to look so troubled? She covered her head and quietly placed the dishes before him. As she served him, she asked, "How is our son-in-law doing?"

"He has typhoid. The doctor expected the fever to break today, but the fever hasn't left him," Somnath said, sighing.

30

"Don't talk on an empty stomach," Bhagya said. She held the edge of her sari between her lips so that her face was all but covered. "Eat something first," she said.

Somnath put a few morsels of rice and plantain curry into his mouth to please her, but he couldn't swallow any more. He sat back, despondently laying his head against the wall. "Hira Lal may be dying," he said. He shut his eyes. "Chuyia's mother-in-law wishes for her son to die at the banks of the Ganges so he can liberate his soul and attain *moksha*. Hira Lal's wife must be at his side. It is the moral thing to do."

"Of course," mumbled Bhagya, sitting stiff, as if she were frozen.

"I will go with them, of course."

Bhagya's rigid body suddenly sank as if it were not only her head but her whole despondent frame that bowed in acquiescence and defeat before her daughter's fate. There was nothing they could say or do in the face of her karma.

"The bullock-cart will be here at dawn," Somnath said gently. "Get Chuyia ready."

Bhagya packed a small tin trunk with Chuyia's favourite skirts and saris, thinking these might be the last days her daughter could wear the bright colours she loved. She placed two squares of almond-fudge *mithai* in a small tin box. If her fate so decreed, such treats would be forbidden to Chuyia.

Later that night, Bhagya allowed her worries and fears to surface. She and Somnath both knew that if Hira Lal managed to recover, Chuyia would be allowed to return home; but if he didn't recover she would be a widow and she would never return to them. Somnath, though numbed with sorrow, was resigned to fulfilling his and his daughter's proper duty to the sick man and his family. Bhagya's thoughts tormented her all night. She knew that in Brahmin culture, once widowed, a woman was deprived of her useful function in society—that of reproducing and fulfilling her duties to her husband. She ceased to exist as a person; she was no longer either daughter or daughter-in-law. There was no place for her in the community, and she was viewed as a threat to society. A woman's sexuality and fertility, which was so valuable to her husband in his lifetime, was converted upon his death into a potential danger to the morality of the community. Bhagya's heart was filled with dread.

Just before Chuyia left, Bhagya lightly slid the kohl applicator between her daughter's sleepy eyelids. Let her daughter look beautiful—she was not a widow yet.

❧

ON THE SECOND DAY of their journey by bullock-cart, Somnath awakened Chuyia before dawn. His voice was sombre, gravelly from staying up. "*Bitya*, change out of your night clothes and roll up your mat." They needed more room to tend to the sick man in their tiny shelter beneath the awning.

Chuyia quickly changed into the brightest colours she could pick out from the tin trunk in the dim light of the oil lamp. She cast a furtive glance at Hira Lal but he was obscured by the shadows cast by her mother-in-law, who was fanning him.

Somnath gave her a long piece of sugar cane, and, delighted by the treat, Chuyia groped her way past the diffused hump of Hira Lal's legs to her narrow perch at the rear of the cart and dangled her feet over the edge. The dawn breeze stirred in her hair and spread it about her in a dark tangle as she dug her teeth into the juicy flesh of the sugar cane. Hira Lal's foot stuck out from under a dirty blue coverlet, and the husk she spat out landed on the arch of his foot and slid down to his ankle. Her head lolling with the movement of the cart, Chuyia drowsily watched the husk cling to the sick man's skin. After a while, she reached over and flicked it off the inert foot. For want of anything better to do, she followed the slow progression of their journey on the deserted road by the trail of white, chewed-out husks she was now careful to spit out as far as she could.

The sun was beginning to rise and already its rays inflamed an oval patch of forest in the distance, while the rest of the forest retained its dark silhouette. As Chuyia swung her feet back and forth, the silver bells encircling her tiny ankles jingled to the rhythm of the cart and she was scarcely aware of Hira Lal's feet as they knocked against her thigh with every dip and turn of the cart.

The dirt road they travelled was slightly elevated, and, between the jungle thickets and the open country, the undergrowth was covered with a trellis of creepers and pierced here and there with coconut trees and banana groves. They overtook a stocky villager with brass pots balanced from a pole slung across his shoulder. Struck by the vibrant colours of Chuyia's red blouse and peacock-blue skirt, the man smiled at the comely apparition the girl made so early in the morning. He noticed the red glass bangles circling her wrists and the smudged mark on her forehead, and concluded that the girl was on her way to her bridegroom's village.

Chuyia, welcoming a diversion, returned his smile and, leaning forward, asked, "What do you have in those pots?"

"Milk," answered the man. "Do you want some?"

Chuyia shook her head, "No," and held out the sugar cane. "You can have it," she offered.

The man laughed, touched by her gesture. "No, child. It's yours. You eat it," he said. His eyes moved from the girl to the murky figures beneath the awning, and he called out a cheerful greeting. But the passengers, hidden by their own long shadows, remained silent.

Turning on his perch behind the bullocks, the young driver returned the villager's greeting and explained, "The travellers are nursing a very sick man, *bhaiya*." His swarthy skin was black from the sun, and he wore a white sleeveless vest open at the chest. "They barely talk—his mother is already grieving. That's his wife." He jerked his head back to indicate Chuyia.

The villager stopped in his tracks. A curious composite of horror and compassion veiled his eyes, as he turned them again to the girl.

"May Bhagwan show them mercy," he said and mumbled a prayer after the receding cart.

As the bullock-cart plodded along the dirt road, Chuyia absently followed the deep ruts its wheels left in the red earth. She had little idea of what she was doing or where she was going. She knew the man they called her husband was sick, and that she was on a journey with him and her dour mother-in-law. So long as *baba* was there to look after her, she felt secure.

Chuyia's attention shifted from the road to the occupants of the bullock cart, and she now became aware of Hira Lal's feet flopping against her. She grew irritated and tried to move away from the contact, but the wooden post at her end of the cart did not allow her the space. Almost hypnotized, she gazed at them: they were large, longer even than Somnath's, and the way the big toes stuck out amused her. But the soles were pale, and not as rough and cracked as her father's. Her husband's feet were accustomed to wearing shoes, she thought, with an unfamiliar touch of pride, and unexpectedly she wanted to claim her husband, to draw the attention of this man who slept all the time and did not play with her. Chuyia quietly lifted the blue sheet and ran a finger down Hira Lal's leg and ankle, and tickled the sole of his foot. Hira Lal's foot twitched slightly. She repeated the action, and so absorbed was she in the game that she didn't notice her father clear his throat in warning.

As if to coax Hira Lal awake, Chuyia, suddenly impatient, rubbed the stick of sugar cane hard against the sole of his foot, and when his leg jumped up reflexively she burst into giggles.

Almost at once a sharp blow struck her head. She turned around, startled. Angered by her inappropriate conduct, Hira Lal's mother had whacked her head with her fan. Chuyia looked at her mother-in-law out of the corner of her eyes, which held the same mildly mocking expression that so infuriated Bhagya. Ignoring the sour old woman, who reminded her of their spiteful neighbour with the fruit orchards, Chuyia calmly bit into her sugar cane as if she didn't have a care in the world.

Chuyia leaned forward to see what lay ahead. There was a bend in the road, and all at once a luxuriant growth of large-leaved water lilies billowed to one side of her like the waves of a green ocean. Here and there, little orange buds thrust up their heads to the sky. Chuyia's senses, attuned to the hues and wonders of nature, quickened to the startling green of the sun-drenched water lilies.

Somnath coughed and cleared his throat, reminding Chuyia of the people behind her. She looked back. The sloping afternoon sunlight filled the cramped space beneath the awning, showing up every detail of the sickroom. Mindful of Hira Lal, she swung her legs clear over him and leaned back against the wooden post to observe what was going on.

Covered by the blue sheet, Hira Lal lay motionless, his eyes closed, his head and shoulders cradled in the folds of Somnath's body. His hair stood up in a brittle tangle, and the oil that had earlier groomed it appeared to have evaporated.

Sitting cross-legged beside him, Hira Lal's mother was applying a wet cloth to his forehead. The stout glass bangles on her wrists tinkled. Every short while she gently raised his head and held a small bowl of water to his lips. Hira Lal could barely sip it. She tenderly wiped the sheen of sweat off his face; her sari had slipped from her head and lay unheeded like a cowl around her neck.

Somnath's crumpled *dhoti* and shirt, and the stubble on his cheeks, made her usually tidy father look like a scruffy labourer. As he wiped his face with the red-checkered scarf around his neck, Chuyia noticed for the first time that his mustache and the hair on his temples had turned grey. For most of the time Somnath's eyes remained closed in prayer. There were deep new lines on his forehead, and it was almost as if the muscles of his face were sagging with the weight of his worries.

The varied forest greens intensified, and, as the sun set, the birds began to twitter. Chuyia watched the day wane. And as the fields, forest and river were muted by the glow of twilight, the bullock-cart arrived at the bank of the Ganges River. The blue-grey waters, dappled by the shadows from overhanging trees, lapped at the shore in tiny ripples. A boatman was waiting for them. The men awkwardly lifted Hira Lal and placed him in a shallow, flat-bottomed boat moored to the shore.

"My trunk," Chuyia cried, looking at her father in alarm.

"Where can we put it, *bitya*?" Somnath said. The boat was filled to capacity. "The cart-driver will take it home," he comforted her.

The boatman pushed his small craft into the river before climbing in, and they all shared the crowded space with Hira Lal's dying body.

There was no room for Hira Lal to stretch out, and he lay propped up on his mother's body, his knees folded to one side. She held on to the boat, and with her free hand steadied her son's head lolling on her chest. The boatman rowed his craft gently, with a single oar, lifting it from one side of the boat to the other to paddle it past eddies and steer it into the central flow of the water.

Chuyia stared across the river as she journeyed into the unknown. She was excited by the unaccustomed sights and, with a child's boundless curiosity, eager to find out what new adventure lay ahead. The beginnings of a town emerged on the other side of the river, and Hira Lal's mother looked at Somnath.

Somnath nodded. "It's Rawalpur: we're almost there."

As the boat picked up speed midstream, small temples with unadorned steeples and domes came into view. The rays of the setting sun burnished the water with gold and ignited the domes. An elongated structure with a paved terrace in front stretched between two temples. Almost at once another came into view, then another, and another, in quick succession. Row upon row of stone steps came all the way down the terraces to the river. Fires shaped like enormous candle flames dotted the terraces at irregular intervals.

"*Baba*, look at the fires," Chuyia exclaimed excitedly.

"Those are the *ghats*," Somnath explained, "where the husks of our earthly bodies are burnt and our souls are consigned to rebirth."

The river turned into a wide ribbon of indigo as dusk faded into night. The fires were blinking and glowing through the trees like large fireflies. The shallow craft seemed to drift across the tranquil waters, and, as Hira Lal's fever-racked heart finally gave out, the boat slowly approached the steps to the *ghats*.

Night enveloped the *ghats* and brought an eerie beauty to the simple rhythm of its configurations. The glistening steps rose from the river to make a border for the earth-platforms, and the adobe walls behind the platforms maintained the symmetry. The numerous *ghats*, self-contained and yet contiguous, were bathed in a reddish glow from the fires and the earth tones of the natural materials infused the red with gold.

Chuyia was almost carelessly disposed of to one side on the top stairs, and quickly forgotten, as the adults made the arrangements for Hira Lal's funeral. Just before leaving, Somnath gave Chuyia his scarf. Exhausted from her journey, confused and frightened at finding herself alone in these strange surroundings, she tucked the scarf under her cheek and almost instantly escaped into sleep on the cold stone steps.

Late in the night, Somnath came looking for her and sat down next to his sleeping daughter, exhausted. He gazed at her as if he wanted to fix her form forever in his memory. Every line in his weary face reflected his grief at her untimely widowhood and the parting that loomed ahead of them like a curse. Finally, giving way to the pain that seemed to have squeezed his heart into something wrung-out and dry, he lay his head on the stone and began to weep, releasing his anguish in half-stifled sobs that racked his body.

After a while, Somnath wiped his face and, composing himself, placed a hand on Chuyia's shoulder. Shaking it gently, bending over her, he said, "*Bitya, bitya*," to rouse the slumbering child.

Chuyia slowly awakened and, pleased to have her father close to her, smiled contentedly. She sat up and rubbed her eyes, smudging the kohl that still lined them.

The soot left hollow shadows that gave her an unbearably forlorn look.

Somnath didn't know how to begin. Groping for words, his voice infinitely kind, he asked, "*Bitya*, do you remember getting married?"

The question was of no great moment to the child, and Chuyia shook her head from side to side. "No," she said in her clear voice.

"Your husband is dead," said Somnath. "You are a widow now."

"For how long, *Baba*?" Chuyia asked.

Somnath looked away, unable to meet her gaze. He could not answer her.

Chuyia was untroubled by her father's pronouncement, having no concept of the impact of those words on her life; so long as he was with her, talking to her so gently, her world was secure.

Hira Lal's mother, Somnath and Chuyia made their way toward the cremation grounds. Hira Lal's body had been prepared for the last rites in one of the warren of rooms behind the adobe façade of the *ghat*. Pallbearers were chanting "*Ram Naam Satya Hai*," "Lord Ram thy name is truth," in the still of the night. Funeral pyres lined the top of the *ghat* platforms, their fires making sinister shapes on the walls. Ash-smeared *sadhus* sat in groups, taking deep drags from their clay ganja-pipes. Funeral attendants, the *doms*, busily fetched firewood from the storage rooms behind the walls and piled it for the cremations, while near the pyres grieving relatives anointed their dead with holy water from the river.

Chuyia watched as two men entered the *ghat*, carrying Hira Lal's body on a bier. His body was wrapped in a white cloth, but his face was exposed. With a child's curiosity, she studied her dead husband. His eyes were closed, and lit by the fires his face appeared to have acquired a ruddy glow; in a sudden flash of memory Chuyia saw him decked out as a groom, and thought, *That was my wedding day.*

The funeral pyre was built on a stone platform with steps leading up to it. The bier was first placed diagonally with Hira Lal's head on the platform and his feet touching the ground below. Then his body was hoisted atop the wooden funeral pyre.

Suddenly, her mother-in-law loomed over Chuyia, and, before Chuyia had time to react, she jerked the *mangal-sutra* off her neck and the beads scattered on the ground. She grasped Chuyia's hand and, using a brick, violently smashed the red glass bangles that hung from her wrist. Then, methodically, with no more concern for the girl than if she were an inanimate object, she took the other hand and with the brick smashed the bangles on her other wrist. Chuyia, struck speechless, looked at her shattered bangles in dismay. She searched her mother-in-law's face with astonished, questioning eyes. But her task accomplished, the aggrieved woman trudged off without a word of explanation or a backward glance. Chuyia realized with a stab of shock that she had ceased to matter to this woman.

The smashing of the bangles was the first of many rituals designed to mark Chuyia's descent into widowhood. One of the hired women attending to their party led

Chuyia through an arch in the wall and into a damp little room. Before Chuyia could protest, the woman pulled down her skirt and pulled her blouse up over her neck and, saying, "You can't wear colours or stitched clothes," threw them in a heap to one side. She hunkered down and in swift, sleight-of-hand motions removed the girl's silver anklets and secreted them on her person. Chuyia stood naked as the day she was born, staring at the vibrant little red-and-blue heap her clothes made. The woman steered her beneath a spigot, and with her rough hands bathed her quickly and dried her with her discarded clothes. Chuyia's skin erupted in goosebumps. Vulnerable and embarrassed, she stared at the woman in mute appeal.

"You are a young one, aren't you?" said the woman staring at her perfectly made little body. "Here," she said, holding out a white length of homespun cloth. "From now on you will have to wear what all widows wear. Come, I'll tie the sari for you."

She wound the cloth around Chuyia and draped it over one shoulder, leaving the other shoulder bare. The sari reached to just below Chuyia's calves. The woman smoothed the cloth over Chuyia's tight little buttocks and thighs, and pulled down the hem. Chuyia lowered her chin and glanced at her small bare shoulder, and the woman tut-tutted. "No blouse. I told you widows are not permitted to wear stitched cloth."

Placing her hand on Chuyia's back, she trotted the newly-minted widow out like a doll she had dressed up for all to see and gloried in their attention as the mildly-shocked mourners turned to stare sympathetically at the comely little widow.

The woman led Chuyia to one of the *ghat's* barbers, a shaggy-haired, scruffy fellow with a fleshy lower lip, who squatted patiently on the steps to one side of Hira Lal's pyre. There was genuine sadness on his face as he examined the child's hair to decide how best to proceed. He had never tonsured such a young widow before. Chuyia turned her large sombre eyes on him, and he smiled at her kindly, then firmly turned her face forward. As he snipped off the first of her long tresses, the barber initiated the next ritual in Chuyia's passage into widowhood.

Having lost all control over what was happening to her, Chuyia sat on the steps stoical and resigned. Deprived of sleep, disoriented by the change in location and the sweep of events she could not comprehend, she was in a daze.

The barber cut her hair in stages. He first cut it to a length of about three inches all over, then, with his swift-moving scissors, he clipped closer and closer to the scalp. With the confidence of a practised artisan, he held up the short tufts of her hair with one hand and, with his scissors, nimbly cropped her hair to within a centimetre of her scalp. Black hair littered Chuyia's bare shoulder and her white sari. She kept her eyes tightly shut. Her fingers involuntarily tore at her sari as the barber held her firmly by the shoulder with one hand and ran his snipping scissors all over her scalp.

Somnath came and sat on the stone step below Chuyia. He had bathed and changed out of his grimy clothes. Resting his head on the palm of his hand, he watched the procedure covertly, through gaps in his fingers; there was an unaccustomed tremor in them, and his face held the cumulative sorrow of all fathers who had watched their young daughters go through this agonizing ritual. It was enforced by the belief that if the widow did not shave her head, every drop of water that fell upon the hair polluted the husband's soul as many times as the number of hairs upon her head.

When there was nothing remaining but fine black stubble, the barber rubbed water all over Chuyia's head. Then he took up a razor and began to drag it inch by inch over her scalp, turning her head gently to reach every area. He rolled up his shirt-sleeve and wiped the residue from the razor on his arm; it was soon covered with a black scum of hair. As the razor scraped across her scalp, Chuyia's teeth were set on edge. Somnath noticed her toes curl, almost reflexively, in mute protest.

His wife had watched her sleeping daughter in the light of the moon and thought that she resembled the moon. Somnath, now looking at Chuyia's round face and shorn head bathed in the glow from her husband's pyre, thought she looked like the dawning sun. The fire outlined the edge of her high forehead and the full curve of her lips, her straight nose and her small chin. With her perfect small features and thick sweeping lashes, she looked unbearably beautiful. A drop of water, grey with stubble, made a trail down the side of her face and ended in the hollow at the base of her neck. Her head, now completely bare and pale, merged with her face to form a perfectly shaped orb.

Hira Lal's pyre had burnt almost halfway down, and the flames darted here and there through the twigs. Out of the corner of his eyes, Somnath saw a man making *pheras* around the burning pyre. He was Hira Lal's older son. He had never seen him before and he never saw him again.

Chapter Four

⋙

Hira Lal's body was cremated just before dawn. Their rituals at the *ghats* completed, the little group trudged through the narrow streets of Rawalpur. Holding a lantern, Hira Lal's mother led the way down the dim alleyways. Chuyia walked silently behind her, clutching a small cloth bundle under one arm. Her feet were bare. Somnath followed closely behind Chuyia, holding a larger bundle and an umbrella with a silver handle. The sounds of roosters crowing and of dogs barking broke the silence. In the pre-dawn darkness, they passed a slightly open door; a slice of light fell through the slit, illuminating the cobbled street and an ancient, dilapidated wall. Chuyia, with the resilience of the very young, was again alive to the new stimuli and looked around her with inquisitive eyes. The walls were pockmarked with patches of brick that showed through the crumbled cement and flaking whitewash. Every instance of architecture appeared to be a crumbling, slowly disintegrating shell of once stalwart structures.

They continued up the cobbled streets until they came to an old building with stray patches of whitewash spared by the elements. A bicycle lay against a broken wall. Chuyia had never seen one before, and she turned to her father. His glance slid past her: it was no time for explanations. A tree grew out of the wall, its entwined willowy trunk crowned by patches of green. Hira Lal's mother led them past it to a door with worn black paint. The walls on either side were marked with inverted swastikas, an ancient holy symbol. She walked up the steps and knocked.

A shadowy figure opened the door to reveal a dark hallway. Hira Lal's mother gestured to them to remain outside, while she followed the figure in. Somnath and Chuyia sat on the front steps, placing their bundles at their sides. Chuyia looked around her, eyes wide with questions. She saw moving figures at the end of the hall where it was lighter, and against her father's protests darted into the hallway and boldly walked down it.

Chuyia pressed a small hand to the wall of a parapet and peered over it into a courtyard. Barely two feet from where she stood, holding a string of wooden prayer beads between her fingers, a woman, who could as easily have been a man, sat on her haunches staring at her. She was very dark, and the thick white fuzz on her tonsured head made a stark contrast. Two ashen lines were drawn perpendicularly from the top of her forehead to a point between her eyebrows, giving her elongated face a fierce aspect. The woman acknowledged Chuyia's presence with a slight nod that appeared to beckon her, as she continued to slowly rock back and forth on her haunches, counting her beads. A small plant sprouted from a crack at the base of a pillar near her. Chuyia vaguely registered the hectic chirrup of sparrows in the courtyard. The woman's mouth was clamped in a sombre line, but her eyes were kind.

Chuyia, terrified by this frightening apparition, turned away and rushed back down the hall to her father, hurriedly saying, "*Baba*, let's go home; *Baba*, let's go home. I don't like this place."

Somnath pulled her down beside him on the step and said, "This is your home now, *bitya*."

Chuyia's face crumpled with disbelief. Cutting through the questions that swirled in her mind, she asked, "Where is *amma*?"

His face heavy with sadness, Somnath turned away, unable to answer his daughter. His lip was drawn in a taut, grieved line, and his chin crumpled beneath it. The flesh beneath his neck hung in a deep fold.

Almost quaking with fear, Chuyia again asked, "*Baba*, where is *amma*?"

Somnath could neither meet his daughter's gaze, nor bring himself to answer her.

Chuyia's voice rose in anger, and she slapped his hand and thigh as she demanded, "*Baba*, *Baba*, where is *amma*?" She could not understand why he didn't answer her.

Hira Lal's mother emerged from the doorway with the widow Kunti. In her early thirties, Kunti had brown skin the colour of creamed coffee and black cropped hair. She stooped to pick up Chuyia's bundle from the stairs, and Hira Lal's mother grabbed Chuyia by the wrist. As Chuyia fought to break free, Kunti, strong and wiry as a whip, clamped her steely fingers around Chuyia's other arm and hoisted the struggling child to her feet. Together, they pulled her up the stairs and through the hallway. Abandoning the howling child to her fate, Hira Lal's mother, blaming the girl for a karmic debt of past sins that had deprived her of her son, trudged back stone-faced and grieving, while Chuyia screamed, "*Baba,* don't leave me here! *Baba,* don't leave me!"

Somnath stood helpless, resigned to his fate and the fate of his daughter. Hira Lal's mother pulled the black panels together and firmly shut the door of the *ashram* on his daughter's fearful cries and on her life.

Somnath turned and led the way, and Hira Lal's mother followed him to the river.

Inside the *ashram,* Chuyia continued to shriek her outrage at finding herself deserted in her strange surroundings. "Let me go! I'm not staying here!" she screamed over and over as Kunti, using both hands, pulled her into the courtyard. A couple of elderly widows who had been tending a tulsi plant sprouting from a concrete planter on the verandah straightened their backs to watch. Another, applying fresh clay to the unpaved courtyard, hastily carried her bucket out of harm's way to a groove beneath a weedy, slanting tree that cut into the verandah roof.

Kunti, grimacing with the effort, held Chuyia by both shoulders as the girl continued to kick and scream. Chuyia managed to free one hand and struck the widow wherever she could. Alternately remonstrating and scolding, Kunti tried to calm her.

The commotion drew the *ashram*'s other residents into the courtyard. Around twenty widows, ranging in age from twenty-five to seventy, emerged slowly and gathered around Kunti and Chuyia. Wraith-like figures in white saris, their every movement seemed to be an apology for their continued existence. They were unadorned except for the two-pronged ash-smears on their foreheads that marked them as devotees of Lord Krishna. With their shaved heads and long, stern faces, some looked like men. They watched in silence as Kunti struggled with the new arrival. Chuyia had by now become quite hysterical.

Suddenly, Chuyia's cries were interrupted by a loud command. "Quiet! Shut her mouth!"

Chuyia was shocked into silence by the power of the voice, and watched in amazement as a large old woman, supported by two widows, emerged from the shadowy recesses. Madhumati hobbled precariously to the *takth*, her accustomed perch in the courtyard, and sat down heavily on the weathered planks. In contrast to the stringy widows, Madhumati had an abundance of slack flesh that made her look much older than her fifty-odd years, and though she wore the same drab white sari as the other widows and her grey hair was as closely cropped to her scalp, she was clearly the ruler of the dilapidated *ashram*.

"Hey, you whore; why haven't you fed my Mitthu?" she shouted at Snehlata, the widow Chuyia now recognized as the mannish-looking person she had seen when she peeped over the parapet wall. The woman was still counting her beads and rocking dispiritedly.

"The poor parrot won't stop squawking."

"*Didi*, there are no lentils," replied a lantern-faced widow, looking up meekly.

"What? No lentils? Then go buy some, you wretch!"
Madhumati shouted. "'No lentils,' she says," she muttered, disgusted.

Madhumati's expressive face underwent a remarkable
transformation as she turned her attention to the bewildered newcomer. Her features softened and her face was
suffused with sympathy, as she smiled fondly and beck-
oned the child to come to her. Chuyia, whose crying had
slowed to an occasional involuntary sob, walked tentatively toward Madhumati.

In a voice surprisingly sweet, Madhumati exclaimed,
"You poor child. How I feel for you! I was also very
young when my bastard husband died! Come! Sit
here."

Hesitantly, Chuyia clambered up onto the ample lap
proffered by Madhumati. It was like scaling a slippery hill. Sweat oozed from Madhumati as from a wet
sponge. She rocked Chuyia gently back and forth on her
lap and stroked her shorn head. Chuyia's breath still
came in short gasps. Continuing to speak in dulcet, sym-
pathetic tones, Madhumati told her, "In our shared
grief, we're all sisters here, and this *ashram* is our only
refuge."

The other widows softly murmured their agreement.
A tear trickled down Chuyia's forlorn face. "I want my
amma," she said on a sobbing intake of breath.

Unmoved by Chuyia's grief, Madhumati continued
her practised spiel. "Our Holy Books say, 'A wife is part
of her husband while he's alive.' Right?"

The widows nodded their heads in solemn concurrence. "And when our husbands die, God help us, the

wives also half die." She paused for effect and sighed dramatically. "So, how can a poor half-dead woman feel any pain?" she asked, not really expecting any answer.

Chuyia, tears still slipping down her face, raised her head, and between sniffles, replied with a child's innocent logic, "Because she's half alive?"

Flaring into a sudden rage, Madhumati heaved herself up from her charpoy and threw the little girl to the ground. Chuyia was stunned and terrified. Looming over her, Madhumati snarled, "Don't try and be too clever with me, or I'll throw you into the river!"

Repulsed and frightened by the grotesque figure standing over her, Chuyia shouted, "I don't want to be a stupid widow! Fatty!" And before anyone knew what was happening, Chuyia darted forward on all fours and dug her sharp teeth into Madhumati's thick ankle. Then she took off, scrambling for her life.

The shocked widows, stunned into inaction by what they had just witnessed, looked dismayed, except for one ancient, sunken-cheeked widow, Patirajji, who was enjoying the spectacle of someone getting the better of the bullying old bat.

Madhumati yelped with pain and screamed after Chuyia, "What did you say? I'll teach you to speak to me like that!" She turned to the immobilized widows. "She bites like a little bitch! What are you corpses staring at? Go. Catch her! Ass-lickers!" she shouted, galvanizing them into a spurt of action.

For the next few minutes, chaos reigned as Chuyia led the women on a wild chase through the courtyard, weaving between the crumbling pillars of the verandah and dodging past them among the few gnarled trees that had survived in this barren place.

Madhumati shrieked, "Are your arms and legs broken? Catch her!"

Kunti and two younger women were making a good effort, but Chuyia eluded their grasp. She escaped through an open door and quickly crouched behind it. Beyond this door the widow Shakuntala was at work, grinding turmeric roots. She looked at the frightened girl speculatively. When Kunti burst into the room and pulled the kitchen door to reveal Chuyia, Shakuntala intervened. "Let her be," she said, with a quiet note of authority that surprised Chuyia.

Kunti stammered, "But...Madhu-*didi* wants—"

Shakuntala looked at her steadily. "Leave," she said.

Kunti, and the other widows who were standing in the door, reluctantly withdrew.

Shakuntala studied Chuyia indifferently, all the while continuing her task.

Crouched behind the door, Chuyia lowered her eyes. She was awestruck. The other widows had deferred to her stern-visaged saviour. She would do well to keep on her good side. Adversity is a rapid teacher.

"Come here," Shakuntala ordered.

Chuyia crawled over to her on all fours and raised her head to look at her with her expressive, questioning eyes. The widow's skin was smooth, and her cropped hair was a black fuzz.

"Sit with your back to me," instructed Shakuntala.

Chuyia did as she was told. Shakuntala took a great yellow glob of turmeric paste from the grinding slab and spread it all over Chuyia's raw scalp. It stung.

"It's turmeric. It cools the head," she said.

With her white sari and bald, yellow head, Chuyia was a very different child from the girl who had ridden in the bullock-cart.

Chuyia turned to face Shakuntala. "You saved me like the Goddess Durga," she said, her eyes round with the beginnings of trust.

Shakuntala turned Chuyia's head back around firmly and continued to apply the paste to the girl's scalp. "Sharp teeth and an even sharper tongue! I'm no goddess. Now go sit in the sun. Go," said Shakuntala, dismissing her. She dipped her fingers into a bowl of coconut oil to remove the dark stains.

Chuyia made no move to go.

Shakuntala spoke impatiently. "Are you deaf?"

After a pause, Chuyia, speaking in a small, fearful voice, said, "They'll throw me into the river!"

"Only if you bite someone else. Now go."

Reluctantly, Chuyia left the sanctuary of Shakuntala's room, but not before she had impishly stuck out her tongue.

Ambling back into the courtyard, Chuyia came upon Patirajji, sitting on the verandah with her back to the pillar. The old widow greeted her with a twinkle in her eyes, and Chuyia got the impression that she had been waiting for her. Chuyia squatted close to Patirajji, as if for protection, ready to spring up at any sign of a widow-attack.

They sat in silence while Patirajji peered at Chuyia short-sightedly. Girlishly formal, she asked, "What's your name?"

"Chuyia."

Shakuntala, concerned for the girl, lifted a ragged yellow curtain to look at Chuyia and Patirajji from her window.

Patirajji made up bit of doggerel and sang:

Chuyia the mouse,
With the sharp little teeth,
And the tight little bite,
Bled the lumpy old louse.

They sat companionably close; the one all angular and withered with age, the other in the bloom of robust childhood. Shakuntala was struck by how appropriate they looked together—similar in their innocence and in their vulnerability, they completed a circle. The very young and the very old belonged together. She let the yellow curtain fall.

Intrigued by the gummy cavern of Patirajji's mouth and impressed by the ditty, Chuyia smiled shyly. "What's your name?" she asked.

"My husband embraced eternity and left behind poor Patirajji. Call me *Bua*, Auntie." Then, mischievously, conspiratorially, holding together the tips of her thumb and forefinger and turning her wrist in a dainty dance movement, she added, "You really made that fat cow dance, didn't you!"

Chuyia, who had not expected kudos for her bad behaviour, smiled bashfully.

"Her family made a donation to a temple in the city: that's why 'Fatty' is the head of the *ashram*," said Bua.

Chuyia absorbed this information. She wondered if Shakuntala-*Didi*'s family had also made a donation. That might explain the authority she had exercised in befriending her.

All at once, with the whimsy lonely old people are apt to cultivate, Patirajji leaned forward on the palms of her hands to gape at Chuyia. "Do you have a *laddoo*?" she whispered hopefully.

Chuyia shook her head, "no."

"Awake or asleep, even in my dreams, all I see are sweets," Bua sighed wistfully.

Chuyia nodded politely. Moved as much by the long, pointy chin and the dipping nose as by her confession, Chuyia felt a surge of affection and pity for the old woman.

Bua got up laboriously with the help of her staff, and, painfully bent, hobbled off to find a warm patch of sun where she could squat and fall asleep.

Since there were no widows about and it was quiet, Chuyia decided to explore her surroundings. She slipped through an open door, and her eyes were immediately drawn to a picture hanging on the opposite wall. It was an oval portrait of a pink-cheeked English girl, clasping a bouquet of flowers in her white hands. She had luxuriant chestnut-brown hair, crowned by a flaming red cap. Even though this strange goddess did not inspire confidence, Chuyia touched the shabby frame and prayed to the image to take her home.

She entered a dingy room and looked about her in the faint light, which leaked in from the courtyard. The plaster was leprous with huge patches of mould. Rickety metal shelves nailed to one side were covered with an assortment of vials. A spigot jutted from another wall, barely visible behind the saris and towels hanging from a string. A few pots were scattered beneath the spigot. She wondered which widow occupied the room.

Chuyia ran lightly across the courtyard. Standing outside a door, she heard snores coming through. She opened the door and peered in.

Stretched out like a beached whale, Madhumati lay flat on an iron bedstead, the bedclothes crumpled in a heap at her feet. A small hookah lay by her side, and some of its contents had spilled on the cotton mattress. A strange odour, mixed with that of tobacco, hung in the fetid air. A window above the head of her bed opened on the alley; it was protected by iron bars. The small room was plastered with pictures of the Hindu pantheon in all its glory. A few white saris were flung on the floor. Hanging in a cage behind Madhumati's bed was Mitthu, her beloved parrot, silently rocking on his perch.

Emboldened by Madhumati's sonorous breathing, and sensing she wouldn't be easily awoken, Chuyia tiptoed to Mitthu's cage and tried to talk to him. Mitthu was a common variety of parrot, his feathers disarrayed from being caged. The parrot's beak dipped like Bua's nose. Chuyia had seen sleek flocks streak greenly between the mango trees in her village, and she felt sorry for this pathetic specimen. "Mitthu, Mitthu, you want a chili pepper?" she crooned. The bird turned a beady eye on her and became still. Chuyia stood on her toes to poke her finger into his fat belly, and Mitthu gave a surprised squawk. The girl glanced at Madhumati, but the woman did not stir. Chuyia tiptoed quietly past her and went back into the courtyard.

Coming to the entrance door, Chuyia gave it a half-hearted tug, expecting it to be locked, but to her surprise it opened. She ran out without shutting it. Almost at once, around a bend, she found herself on a noisy street, teeming with life. A leprous beggar sitting cross-legged on a platform on the busy sidewalk calmly wiped his partially collapsed face with a cloth. The cement plaster on the walls that lined the street was covered with advertisements, displaying medicine vials and posters with Hindi lettering. Large patches of cement had fallen off the walls, and the exposed brick beneath was white from the brackish damp that seemed to afflict the old buildings.

Hearing a clamour of bells and some voices rising in unison, Chuyia turned into a street to investigate the source and discovered a temple hall where a daily service provided by the widows was taking place. She spotted the *ashram* women here and there in the thicket of widows dancing in the centre. Frequently, a seated widow would get up to dance, and an exhausted dancer would flop down among the squatters. No wonder the *ashram* was quiet and she'd had the run of the place. Where had all the other widows sprung from? There must have been at least a thousand widows and they must have come from other *ashrams* in the town. The anemic-looking widows were clapping as they pleased, singing and swaying clumsily without any effort to keep time. The entire performance was so joyless that it was frightening. The widows' discordant voices mingled with ringing temple bells, and, suddenly, Chuyia's senses were overwhelmed by the sadness emanating from the croaking voices. She ran back to the relative sanctuary of the *ashram*.

Some days later, Chuyia learned that she was living in a singing *ashram*-temple. The widows sang Lord Krishna's and Radha's names to bless their benefactors and grant the requests of supplicants to cure a sick person, or get a job, or to benefit their business. They paid the temple priests, and the widows were given a cup of rice and a fistful of lentils for every eight-hour session of singing and dancing. For many widows, this was their only means of sustenance. On those days when a widow was too sick to perform, she starved.

Chapter Five

✖

Shakuntala was drawing a battered bucket of water from a well in the *ashram* courtyard. She stood where the brick parapet surrounding the well had come undone and the wall was low, allowing easier access to the water.

"So you're back?" said Shakuntala, indifferent and at the same time knowing.

Chuyia was humiliated. Shakuntala guessed that she had run off and then returned of her own volition. She did not reply.

Shakuntala offered her a drink of water, but Chuyia sullenly refused. Shakuntala shrugged her shoulders as if to say, "As you wish," and returned to her room. Only then did Chuyia go to the well and, pouring the water from a pot into her cupped hand, drank thirstily. She was washing her face when she felt something drop on her head. She ignored it, but when a second pebble hit the brick beside her, her attention was drawn and she looked up. At the top of a narrow stairway she had not noticed before, there stood a stunningly beautiful young woman, motioning to Chuyia to join her. Her head, Chuyia immediately noticed, was not shorn. Chuyia looked about her, wondering what to do. There was no one to instruct her.

The young woman, who couldn't be more than nineteen or twenty, nodded encouragingly as Chuyia, awestruck, slowly made her way up the stairs. A coil of dark hair knotted at the back framed the bright oval of her face, and a tail from the knot fell to her waist. When Chuyia neared the top of the stairs, Kalyani held out her hand and pulled her onto a balcony. Her eyes, wide beneath the thick arches of her brows, were friendly and kind. They were the shape and colour of almonds. To Chuyia, she seemed like an angel.

They were on the flat terrace of the *ashram* above Madhumati's room. A decaying wooden balustrade ran along the balcony. Kalyani led Chuyia to her room. It was a small storeroom that Madhumati had had cleaned out and allotted to her a few months after she had arrived at the *ashram*. A barred window offered a view of the Holy City below, with its crowded jostle of temples, old buildings, minarets and mosques. Kalyani led Chuyia over to a corner of the room and told her to sit down on a mat. She fetched a deep wicker basket and, settling down cross-legged, raised the lid slightly. With an air of mystery, as if she was a conjurer, she put her hands in the basket, and told Chuyia, "Close your eyes."

Chuyia blinked, confused.

"Close them tight!" Kalyani said, squeezing her own eyes shut to show her how.

Chuyia followed Kalyani's example.

Smiling in anticipation of the joy she would bring the child, Kalyani pulled a small mongrel puppy from the basket and deposited him on Chuyia's lap. "His name is Kaalu," she told her.

The puppy licked Chuyia's face. He had short black fur with patches of white on his chest and paws. His ears were soft and floppy. Totally captivated, Chuyia cradled the puppy close to her face, kissing him and murmuring into his soft fur, "Kaalu, Kaalu." She was swamped by the same feelings of happiness and tenderness that had welled up in her when she had found Tun-tun in the forest, and holding his softness to her flesh, carried him home. For the first time since she had left home, Chuyia found something that brought her joy.

"You can play with him any time you want," Kalyani offered. She untied the knot at the corner of her white sari and took out a dried *chapati*. She gave it to Chuyia, saying, "You feed him."

Chuyia tore the *chapati* into small bits and fed the eager little dog, while Kalyani looked at both of them affectionately.

"He has fleas," Kalyani admitted. "I should bathe him."

"Downstairs? By the well?" Chuyia asked.

Kalyani, laughing, said, "No! They think dogs are a bad omen. Don't tell anyone I have Kaalu up here. It's our secret."

Chuyia nodded her solemn concurrence. Kaalu, having eaten the *chapati*, climbed out of Chuyia's arms. They followed his antics, laughing. Suddenly Kaalu rolled over on his back and, with his little white-tipped paws suspended in the air, fell fast asleep.

"This is just what Tun-tun used to do," cried Chuyia, hugely excited.

"Tun-tun was your puppy?" Kalyani asked, as she placed Kaalu back in the straw-lined basket.

"He is big now," Chuyia said.

"You miss him?" Kalyani asked.

Chuyia nodded.

"When you think of Tun-tun, come upstairs. We'll both play with Kaalu."

"But I'm not staying here," Chuyia told Kalyani, speaking in all seriousness. "My mother's coming to get me."

Kalyani did not reply.

"If not today, tomorrow for sure," added Chuyia defiantly.

Kalyani walked across the room and drew back a limp saffron curtain to reveal a tiny shrine to Lord Krishna and his consort, Radha. Two brass trays sat on a chipped stone shelf. One tray held a clay incense holder with half-burned sticks of incense jutting out of the perforations, a small pot with ash and other religious artifacts. The other tray, with a tiny brass Krishna attached to its rim, also supported a larger statue of Krishna playing his flute and fresh marigold flowers. He wore a pink shawl, and his head was framed by a pink halo. A bright green feather extended from the halo. Greenery peeped in through the window behind the shrine, and sunlight drenched the lemony marigold flowers at Krishna's feet. A blue cloth bundle hung from a nail on the wall nearby, and Chuyia wondered what was in it.

Kalyani pressed her hands together and addressed the statue. "Krishna, this is my friend…" She turned to Chuyia and asked, "What's your name?"

"Chuyia," replied the little girl. Then, in awe, she asked, "Can he hear you?"

"Of course—he hears everything!"

Kalyani bowed down and prostrated herself before the shrine. She swept her hands on the floor and lightly rubbed the dust on her face. She clasped her hands in front of her and shut her eyes. Almost at once, she appeared to be immersed in deep meditation. After a while, Kalyani bowed her head to salute the god and opened her eyes. She smiled and turned to Chuyia.

"What did he say?" Chuyia asked uncertainly.

"He says you won't be here long."

"I told you so," Chuyia replied confidently.

"You must do *japa*. Chant *Jai Shree Krishna* 108 times a day, and soon you'll fly away home," Kalyani advised.

Worried, Chuyia said, "But I can only count to ten."

Kalyani gave Chuyia a string of beads and said, "This has 108 beads. Why don't you start the *japa* now?"

Chuyia began to chant in earnest, "*Jai Shree Krishna...Jai Shree Krishna...*"

MOONLIGHT STREAMED IN from the open door and silvered the white outlines of the widows lying on the floors of two haphazardly connected rooms. They lay on their mats, chanting, coughing, snoring, moaning and filling the night with troubled sounds. Chuyia lay wide-eyed on her mat, muttering "*Jai Shree Krishna, Jai Shree Krishna,*" as much to drown out the scary noises the women made as to work the magic of the mantra that would fly her home. Suddenly, a figure crouched down by her mat, startling her, and Chuyia sat up. It was Shakuntala. She told her to roll up her mat and follow her.

In Shakuntala's room there was only Bua, curled up on her mat and fast asleep at the other end of the room beneath the small window with the frayed yellow cloth that served as a curtain. After instructing Chuyia to spread her mat and sleep next to the old woman, Shakuntala settled down on the floor before a religious text that lay open on a low table. She covered her head with a white cloth and, adjusting the oil lamp, began to read. Every short while, she closed her eyes to dwell on the spiritual message contained in the scriptures. Shakuntala had never questioned the belief in the *Dharma Shastra* that widowhood was the punishment for a sinful existence in the past, and she atoned for it with prayer and the observance of fasts as prescribed. Focusing on studying the scriptures and trying to live as purely as possible, the obligation to pray constantly in penance for her husband's death brought her solace. It also dulled the pain of the memories of all she had lost and all she had endured.

About two years earlier, Shakuntala had brought Bua to her room to nurse her through a bout of malaria, and the old woman had slept there ever since. Chuyia lay down next to her. After tossing restlessly for a while, she propped up her head and tried to see if Auntie was awake. Moonlight filtered through the curtain and fell softly on the widow. Bua lay absolutely still, eyes shut, breathing evenly. Her suspicions aroused by the regular breathing, Chuyia remained at her post, vigilant. Her attention must have wandered for a split second, because all at once she noticed that Bua's eyes were wide open. Chuyia wiggled closer to her and accusingly whispered, "I knew you were awake!"

Bua sat up, cackling with delight at having played a joke on her new friend. She had the straight-backed posture of a slender young girl. Delighted by the presence of this unexpected night companion she could talk to, Bua soon began reminiscing about her life in her village and the mischief she and her sisters would cook up at the village pond.

Bua talked about her mother, narrating with relish the gory details of the severe thrashings her sisters and she received when they were caught stealing corn from their neighbour's fields.

This Chuyia could relate to; she launched into her own account of her escapades in her sour neighbour's mango orchard, and the vigorous thrashing she routinely received from her mother. Bua listened with interest, and every now and again responded with a flattering cascade of cackles. Bua told her how she and her younger brother were once lost in the forest for two days and a night. Despite the difference in their ages, and the distance between their villages, Bua's childhood had been much the same as Chuyia's.

Bua began to describe her wedding ceremony, and Shakuntala, sitting at her low desk, looked up from the book. She smiled, knowing where the conversation would lead to, as all conversation with Bua inevitably did. "While the priest was reciting the vows," Auntie told Chuyia, "I started to laugh. I knew I shouldn't, but I couldn't help it. I had a fit of laughter. I pulled my veil forward to hide my face and laughed. Some women thought I was sobbing, and they began to sob. This made me laugh even more. Suddenly, Ma slapped me hard, and then, till the end, not a squeak from me!"

Bua paused to gauge the effect of her story on the girl. Chuyia, hugely entertained, was grinning from ear to ear.

"And after the wedding ceremony—" Bua's mouth seemed to fill with saliva. "Afterwards…"

Here it comes, thought Shakuntala, looking up from the book. But Chuyia interrupted instead. "I know what happened afterward."

"What?" asked Bua.

"The wedding feast!" Chuyia declared.

"Yes…You should have seen the sweets," Bua said, and launched into the expected spiel.

"Plump white *rasgullas*, piping hot *gulab jamuns*. The saliva drools in my mouth even now when I think of it! Yellow *laddoos*, fragrant with saffron, dripping with pure butter. Cashew-nut fudge covered with gold leaf…" Bua trailed off in ecstasy.

Chuyia, transported to the past by Bua's dream-like description, was silently weeping. Bua edged closer, peering at her through the darkness. "Hush, child hush," she said softly, and with her weak, claw-like grasp tried to draw Chuyia to her. Wiggling forward on her elbows, Chuyia buried her face in Bua's ribby bosom. Bua stroked Chuyia's small, bare shoulder, her back, her cropped hair, until the heaving of the little body next to her subsided to an occasional shudder, and the distressed child drifted off to sleep.

Bua sighed, and then observed to no one in particular, "Life is so disappointing."

Shakuntala, who had been concerned for the child and watched while Bua soothed her, raised an eyebrow and, impervious to Bua's depressingly truthful observation, continued reading.

Some time later that night, Chuyia was awakened by Bua's gasping snorts and snoring. The lamp was out, and she rolled back to her mat. She could just make out the dim outline of the little mound Shakuntala made, as she slept near her reading table. Lying flat on her back, her eyes shut tight, Chuyia began to do the *japa*. "*Jai Shree Krishna...Jai Shree Krishna...*"

Chapter Six

≋

Chuyia sat on the steps, playfully kicking up the water. Nearby, knee-deep in the shallows, Kalyani was bent over, vigorously soaping Kaalu. The little dog squirmed and barked. "Stay still, you rascal," Kalyani scolded. She included Chuyia in her playful glance as she splashed water on Kaalu and muttered, "We must get rid of your fleas...Sins, too, while we're at it."

Close to them a grey-haired woman was absorbed in a washing and prayer ritual. She appeared not to notice them.

"There," Kalyani said, hauling Kaalu out of the water and holding him aloft. "Both fleas and sins washed away!"

Chuyia laughed out loud, and the woman turned around. Kalyani began to murmur an apology, but the woman, realizing they were widows, glared at her in a way that made Kalyani blush and stop mid-sentence, guiltily clutching at her wet sari. Clasping Kaalu to her chest, Kalyani waded up the steps and sat down next to Chuyia. Kaalu yelped and whined as he tried to get away, and Chuyia burst out laughing.

"Chuyia! Stop laughing!" Kalyani whispered fiercely.

Chuyia was perplexed. "Why?" she asked.

"Why what!" Kalyani said impatiently. The woman had moved further upstream. "Give me the towel."

Chuyia handed over the frayed blue-and-white cotton cloth. Kalyani, keeping a firm grip on the whimpering and wriggling Kaalu, rubbed him thoroughly, trying to scour the fleas off his hide.

"Kalyani," Chuyia cried, "you're hurting him!"

Alarmed by Chuyia's distress, Kalyani flung the towel aside. She gently stroked the dog's wet fur with her hand. Her lovely shoulders were limp, and, for just a moment, Chuyia glimpsed of kind of apathy in her eyes that she had not noticed before, the same resignation that dimmed the eyes of the other widows.

"Let me wipe him," Chuyia said, extending her arms toward Kaalu. Kalyani hesitated. He was becoming difficult to restrain. "Be careful," she said, handing the puppy over, but Kaalu, grasping the opportunity, leapt from her arms and bounded up the steps.

"Kaalu!" Chuyia cried in panic, and immediately raced off after the dog, following him quickly up the steps. She waited for an instant by the arching wall of a small Shiva temple for Kalyani to catch up, and then ran off behind it and down the steps on the other side.

Her wet hair flying behind her, widow-decorum out the window, Kalyani ran in frantic pursuit of Chuyia, yelling, "Come back! He won't get lost," and slammed into a stout, colourfully attired woman returning from the river. The woman groped at Kalyani, trying to keep her balance, but immediately released her. "What filth!" she hissed, an ugly expression distorting her harsh features. "You have no shame." Huge loop earrings dangled from her ears, and she had a damp towel over a shoulder. A *mangal-sutra* necklace that cut into her neck and the outsized *bindi* blazing between her brows proclaimed her married status. She grabbed Kalyani by the arm and said, "You have no morals! You are a widow, and yet you run around like you are an unmarried girl?" Then she yanked her arm away as if she'd been stung and hissed, "You've polluted me. I have to bathe again!" She retraced her steps to the river.

Chastened, Kalyani lowered her head and pulled the *pallav* edge of her sari right down to the tip of her nose: if she could, she would have burrowed into the earth.

Chuyia and Kaalu had disappeared. Kalyani sat down on the edge of a stone bench that circled the enormous trunk of a majestic old banyan tree in front of the steps leading up to the Shiva temple. She waited patiently; Chuyia would have to pass this way to get to the *ashram*.

HOT IN PURSUIT OF KAALU, Chuyia raced past the temples that lined the river and down a narrow lane, scattering a cluster of hens and disturbing a magnificently feathered rooster, who squawked haughtily after her retreating back. She ran right through a batch of brilliant red peppers spread out to dry on a mat, scattering them in all directions, and rounded a corner onto a busy city street. She kept calling urgently, "Kaalu! Kaalu!" and, as she ran past a stall where a customer sat drinking tea, the cashier, standing behind burlap sacks of onions and potatoes and stands of coconut and plantains, shouted after her, "Go back to the *ashram*, child." The customer shook his head and remarked, "They shouldn't allow widows to run around like this. They bring bad luck to our business."

Chuyia had almost caught up to Kaalu when he suddenly stopped to sniff at the sandal-clad feet of a handsome young gentleman.

Susceptible to beauty in all its forms, Chuyia gaped round-eyed at the splendid man. He wore a sparkling white *dhoti* with long, graceful pleats in front, and a white shirt. His thick black hair, gleaming with oil and slicked back, reached to his collar. He had heavy, artfully arched eyebrows above wire-rimmed glasses that gave him a learned air. His strong features were set off by a close-cropped moustache and his square jaw by the shadow of a beard. He carried a black umbrella and coat under one arm and a brown suitcase in the other.

Chuyia, already out of breath from her run, found she couldn't breathe. When she could, she quickly gasped, "Catch Kaalu! Please, sir, catch Kaalu!"

Looking kindly at the pup, and more than slightly amused, the young man put his suitcase down and picked up the dog. The umbrella and coat maintained their location beneath his arm.

Chuyia, twisting shyly on one leg, rewarded him with a beaming smile. He handed the puppy over to her and picked up his valise. Chuyia hugged Kaalu tight to her.

"Is he yours?" asked the smiling young man.

Chuyia nodded. "Yes." Attempting to explain the situation, and at the same time to hold his attention, she said, "Yes, Kaalu. He doesn't like to bathe."

The man accepted her explanation and was about to walk away when the dismayed expression on Chuyia's face stopped him.

"What's wrong?" he asked.

"I'm ... I mean ... Kalyani's lost," stammered Chuyia, reluctant to admit that it was she, in fact, who was lost.

"We should find her, then," the man replied matter-of-factly, as if he knew exactly whom Chuyia was talking about.

"Yes, poor thing," said Chuyia.

"Where did she get lost?" the man inquired casually.

"Near the river; by the Shiva *mandir*."

Walking side by side, they started down the street. The man held out a protective arm as a nonchalant cow brushed past them. Oblivious of the traffic, a tailor ironed clothes on a table out on the sidewalk. Chuyia's companion had to duck to get past the clothes the tailor had strung up, and she got a closer look at his face.

They walked quietly. "I'm a widow," Chuyia solemnly confessed. She kept a tight hold on Kaalu as she looked at him.

The man simply said, "Yes. I know."

"How do you know?" Chuyia asked shyly.

The man stopped. He bent down and ran a light hand over the stubble on her head. "That's how," he said, smiling into her eyes. Chuyia blushed. "What's your name?" he asked.

"Chuyia," she said pertly.

"Little mouse!" The young man laughed.

Chuyia shrugged her shoulders; it was a reaction she often elicited from grown-ups when they heard her name. Chuyia turned her face up. "What's your name?" she asked.

"Narayan."

Chuyia, giving him a playful look, sang out, "Narayan-Narayan—like Vishnu's Narayan?"

"Yes," Narayan wryly replied.

They walked in companionable silence until they arrived at the Shiva-*lingam* temple. Chuyia ran across the temple and looked down. Kalyani was there, waiting for her and Kaalu beneath the huge tree. Chuyia walked carefully down the steps with Kaalu in her arms and cried out, "Kalyani!"

Narayan had noticed the demure figure sitting on the stone bench under the great spread of the banyan. Her head was draped in white, and she was framed by the golden leaves strewn around her. The leaves fanned out behind her, reaching down the steps, right up to the water.

Turning her head at Chuyia's voice, Kalyani stood up. She was too relieved to see Chuyia to scold her, and the words she had rehearsed vanished as Chuyia ran up to her and placed Kaalu into her arms. "I found him! Kalyani, I found him!" Chuyia said, chattering in her excitement.

"You silly girl," Kalyani said, drawing the girl close. "Do you know how worried I was? What if you'd got lost? What would I have done then?"

Chuyia suddenly remembered Narayan and his role in finding not only Kaalu but also Kalyani. She looked guiltily up at him as he came down the *mandir* steps and joined the little group.

Kalyani, as yet unaware of Narayan, gently reprimanded Chuyia. "Always running around like your little
namesake, the mouse!"

But Narayan was all too aware of Kalyani. He stood
transfixed, completely enchanted, and stared at her as if
she were the first woman created by God. As Kalyani
became aware of Narayan's presence, she broke off in
mid-sentence and took on a reproving and suspicious
mien. A young man had no business lurking so close
to women he didn't know. Chuyia realized she needed to
explain his presence. Reluctant to see her glory in catching Kaalu diminish, she began a hesitant introduction.

"Kalyani...Narayan helped me find Kaalu."

Their eyes met. His intense, handsome face and the
adulation transparent in his eyes left her feeling breathless
and weak. She wanted to conceal the powerful effect he
had on her but couldn't: she appeared to have no control
over her facial muscles, and her body was responding of
its own accord.

Narayan was struck mute, mesmerized by the contours of Kalyani's perfect face, which at that moment was
being licked enthusiastically by Kaalu.

Kalyani, completely flustered, could neither speak nor
remove her eyes from his. Then, pulling herself together
with monumental effort, she said, "Come, Chuyia." She
held Kaalu close to her and began to walk away. Chuyia
followed her, and Narayan, a few steps behind them,
walked as if he knew he shouldn't, but couldn't help it.

Awkwardly, haltingly, he addressed their receding
backs, "Please...Where do you live?" At once aware
of the impropriety of the question, he tried again. "I

mean...I'm not asking where you live, but—asking if you're lost. I could take you where you live..." he trailed off lamely, embarrassed by his own incoherence.

Chuyia, bewildered by the hesitation in this speech and this uncertainty in the man who had been so assured, stared at him. Then she noticed the helpless way he was looking at Kalyani, and, noting Kalyani's expression, which had by now softened in amusement, Chuyia took pity on him. "She lives in the House of Widows," she said. "I'm just visiting her."

Kalyani, prohibited by tradition from addressing a stranger directly, spoke to Narayan through Chuyia.

"Chuyia, tell him not to follow us. It'll be a sin."

Obligingly, Chuyia turned to him and said, "Don't follow us. It'll be a sin."

Narayan, looking helpless and increasingly desperate, asked, "But where is the House of Widows? Can you tell me?"

"I don't know," Chuyia replied casually.

With a gesture of his head to indicate Kalyani, Narayan said, "Ask her if she knows."

Chuyia obediently addressed Kalyani and repeated, "Ask her if she knows."

She was enjoying this.

Kalyani smiled ever so slightly. Then, speaking in a barely audible voice, she said, "Dharma Ghat."

"Dharma Ghat," Chuyia repeated.

"Beside the river," Kalyani added under her breath.

"Beside the river," Chuyia said to Narayan.

As Chuyia and Kalyani continued to walk away from Narayan, he stood, powerless to stop them. In a daze, he traced his path back to the banyan with its golden spread of fallen leaves and, sitting on the stone bench beneath it, abandoned himself to the confusing and at the same time joyous onslaught of his feelings.

NARAYAN BOUNDED UP THE STEPS and through the front door of the house into the main foyer. Juthika Roy's sweet voice, singing a *bhajan* in praise of Lord Krishna, drifted down from above. It was his mother's favourite record, and she never tired of playing it on their new wind-up gramophone, taking care to change the needle every time.

"Ma!" he called.

Bhagwati hastily set aside her stitching and all but ran through the polished marble hallway. Narayan watched her glide down the stairs, barely touching the mahogany balustrade, as she hurried down to greet him. Her hair was still dark, and she looked trim and pretty in a sari that reflected the blue sky outside the French windows.

Bhagwati's eyes shone, and her entire face had lit up. She reached out her hands, too choked up with emotion to say anything. Narayan put his valise down where he stood and, taking a few steps forward, bent to touch his mother's feet. She blessed him and, as he straightened, she seized his arms. It always surprised her how tall he was. The muscles beneath his shirt felt pleasantly taut. "God bless you, my son. I've been waiting for you all day," she said, when she could speak. "I thought you had changed your mind and wouldn't show up at all." Her voice still throbbed with the disappointment she had felt when he didn't turn up at the time he was expected to. "What happened?! Was the train late?"

"Yes," Narayan said. Uneasy with the lie, he added, "I stopped in town to look for some books."

Narayan was in fact about to go into a bookshop when Kaalu had sniffed him out on the street, and Chuyia had appealed to him for help. He sent up silent thanks to a benign providence that had guided Kaalu to him. He had done this several times since he had seen the gorgeous widow.

"Well, I've been waiting to hear all day. How did your exams go? Pass or fail?" his mother asked.

Narayan shook his head sadly, with such a morose expression that she stepped back in alarm. "Double fail," he said, before breaking into a smile.

Bhagwati slapped him playfully on the cheek and hugged him once again. "Rascal! You'll never change!" she said. "Live long! Be happy!"

Narayan clasped her in a hug and lifted her off the floor. Up close there was grey in her hair.

Narayan went to his room shortly afterward. He set his briefcase on the bed. It was a four-poster with a canopy on top to hold mosquito netting. The room was small with sparse, utilitarian furnishings, a departure from the elaborate furniture filling the rest of the house. Simple curtains hung at a narrow, floor-to-ceiling-length window. One wall was lined with shelves packed with books and a small fan to cool him during his studies. The wall above the shelves was covered with framed diplomas, attesting to his scholarship. As Narayan opened his briefcase, the family servant, Sadhuram, entered the room, carrying his suitcase and umbrella, which he set on the table.

"Master, should I unpack for you?" he asked.

"No need, I'll take care of it," Narayan replied.

Sadhuram looked crestfallen. "As you wish, Chhotay Babu," he said, going to the window to draw the curtains.

As he turned to leave, Narayan stopped him. He rummaged through his pockets and dug out a coin. He gave it to Sadhuram, saying, "Don't get drunk with this, Sadhuram*ji*."

Sadhuram accepted the coin and then turned away, seeming indignant but smiling nonetheless. Narayan had always been kind to him. "My hands haven't touched the bottle for years."

"Make sure your lips don't, either," Narayan said, his mouth twitching into a grin.

Sadhuram left the room. Narayan opened his briefcase and carefully removed a framed picture. He held it gingerly, as though it were a relic. Inadvertently, he bowed his head as he wiped the glass with his shirt sleeve. He removed an old school portrait crowded with stiff replicas of his classmates from the wall and replaced it with the new picture. It was a photograph of a *khaddar*-clad Gandhi, leaning on his staff. Narayan stood in front of the newly hung photo, pleased with its effect in his spartan room.

Chapter Seven

The eunuch, Gulabi, did not walk; she sashayed. She lived in a colony of eunuchs on the outskirts of the city and, like most of them, served in various widows' *ashrams* in some capacity or other.

Hips swaying, arms moving sinuously as she progressed, Gulabi sang and hummed all the way along the dark alley. Despite her girth and musculature, Gulabi was surprisingly graceful. What she lacked in feminine beauty, she more than made up for in ornate dress. She wore a white blouse with shiny red trim, a jade-green sari, dangling earrings, a cuff bracelet and multiple ornaments in her black hair, which was oiled and pulled back from her hatchet-like face into a matronly bun. Just before reaching Madhumati's window, she turned her head back over one shoulder and spat a red stream of betel juice without breaking stride.

Madhumati, slack-faced and glum, propped up against the metal rungs of the headboard, sat sprawled on her bed. Her face glistened with sweat as she fanned herself with a brooding air of abstraction. Although the occasional breeze coming in through the window brought little relief from the heat, it blithely carried the buzz and hum of Gulabi's tuneless ditties. Mitthu's cage was covered with a dark cloth; the light from the lantern hanging over Madhumati's bed got him squawking. The only other light came from a candle flickering on a shelf beside the bed.

Gulabi arrived at Madhumati's window humming, reached both hands through the bars and began to massage and scratch her greasy grey head in a manner reminiscent of the friendly grooming carried on by monkeys. After a while, Madhumati let out a protracted, appreciative sigh, and divested herself of the dark thoughts that had been occupying her mind. "It was the night of *Maha Shivratri* when I was born. In the morning, when my father was allowed to see me, it was love at first sight for Thakur Nirender Ray! He named me Madhumati: 'golden-hued.'"

"You were truly 'golden-hued,'" agreed Gulabi. Madhumati cast her a baleful glance, and Gulabi good naturedly added, "You still are."

"Thakur Nirender went against the wishes of his entire family and brought me up as a son! I was the true Queen Bee. I had a kind heart then. I asked my father for money and never spent it on myself; I gave it all to the beggars and widows.

"When the family forced him to get me married, he gave me a dowry like I was a king's daughter! Where is the king's daughter now? In this dung-heap!"

Gulabi, massaging Madhumati's head through the bars, made appropriate clucking sounds of sympathy. When Madhumati was in this mood, it was best to let her have her say. She would wind down, and once she'd had her fix she would be better company.

"My heart has become hard," Madhumati said, thumping the top of her chest like a hollow drum. "Feel it." She reached back to grab Gulabi's hand and hauled it to the vicinity of her bosom. "See? Feel it. See how hard it is?"

Taken aback, Gulabi felt her arm wrenched against the bars and her hand sink through the spongy flesh to Madhumati's hard ribs. She shrieked, "*Didi*, you're tearing my arm off!"

Madhumati let go of her hand. "My husband, the old bastard, was so horny. The minute he climbed on me, instead of coming, he went! Straight to heaven! Bastard! Pleasuring himself in heaven...And me, stuck in this hell!"

Massaging her sore armpit, Gulabi tut-tutted. Then she leaned closer to Madhumati and huskily whispered, "Poor man!"

Madhumati, vaguely aware she had just been insulted, turned to glare at Gulabi. "Poor who?"

Gulabi slickly placated her. "Poor you, I mean."

"Yes," said Madhumati, allowing her head to rest back. "Poor me. I was brought up to give orders and command all my life. That is why I could stand up to that *haram zadi* mother-in-law of mine when I became a widow! I boldly asked for part of my dowry and some ancestral property to live off of. The bitch foamed at the mouth and threw a fit. I fought back, demanding what was mine! 'Take care of this brazen hussy!' she told her sons. They took care of me, all right! The two bastards raped me for a week. I was shorn and beaten and taken twenty miles into the wilderness and discarded!" Madhumati began to cry. "I don't know what would have happened to me if you hadn't found me."

"We were fated to meet, so I found you," said Gulabi.

This didn't appear to please Madhumati. "Whether we were fated to meet or not, I was fated to live," she corrected.

Gulabi had been foraging for firewood with two other eunuchs when they spotted the shorn creature, covered in blood and half-dead from starvation, lying in a ditch on the edge of the forest. They could tell from the patches of dried blood and her torn clothes that the girl had been raped. They had brought her to the *ashram* in Dharma Ghat. This was almost forty years ago. Madhumati, like Gulabi, was barely fourteen at the time.

The elderly widow who headed the *ashram* had helped Madhumati abort the fetus resulting from rape. She had allowed the girl's hair to grow and had nourished her back to health. At the end of two months, she asked an older eunuch to take the girl to a "client."

Madhumati took charge of the *ashram* when the widow became sick and, through a shrewd combination of charm and gumption, established herself as the ruler of the house when the widow died. The other widows deferred to her and accepted her leadership even though she was only twenty-four years old at the time. What is more, Madhumati had persuaded an influential "client" to bring pressure to bear on her husband's family, and they had been forced to relinquish a part of her inheritance as a donation to the *ashram* temple.

Gulabi decided to change the subject. She was dying to impart the latest bit of information the eunuch grapevine had brought her. Clasping the bars, she rammed as much of her garishly made-up face as she could between them to share the latest gossip.

"*Didi*, have you heard?" Gulabi asked in her deep, affected voice.

"What?"

"About that Mohandas?" she said.

"Mohandas who? Is he a new client?"

"No, Mohandas Gandhi! He's from the jungles of Africa. He doesn't sleep, he doesn't drink."

"Why? Doesn't he feel sleepy?"

"Nooo! He doesn't sleep with women. He lies besides them, but he doesn't sleep with them. Self-discipline, he says."

"No!" exclaimed a disbelieving Madhumati. Jolted into relative alertness by this startling news, she suddenly realized that Gulabi had been idling far too long. She barked, "Why are you still here? Take her to Seth Dwarkanath. It's already late. Standing here gossiping with me—" With a change in tone she said, "Hand it over."

Gulabi rummaged in a satin pouch hooked to the waistband of her sari and brought out a small metal pipe packed with marijuana. She struck a match, lit the pipe, stylishly raised it to her mouth and inhaled several puffs to get it going. Then she placed it in the hand Madhumati was impatiently wagging at her. Madhumati held the pipe to her mouth with both hands, closed her eyes and immediately took several deep, long drags.

"Long live Lord Shiva!" she said, banishing her gloomy mood with an ecstatic sigh.

Gulabi sidled off down the alley, awkwardly wagging her hips and humming and singing.

⊰⊱

NARAYAN SAT ON THE *ghat* steps, playing the haunting evening *raag, Darbari,* on a wooden flute. His friend Rabindra reclined on the step below him, drinking from a silver flask and nodding his head appreciatively, as the sweet notes filled the air. He was dressed Western-style with dark slacks, loafers and a shirt-collar left unbuttoned at the top.

Although night had obliterated the river, the *ghats* were well lit from the ovals of orange that flared intermittently along the walls. Beneath them, two men tended a funeral pyre; the mourners stood to one side, watching quietly. A cow, blurred by the night and looking as if carved from granite, stood above the flight of stairs. A soft chorus of crickets chirruped in the trees, supplying an accompaniment to Narayan's melody: from far off came the broken drift of a song carried in snatches by the breeze.

A lone light glided slowly down the river. As the small boat, which was the source of both the bobbing light and the song, drew closer, Rabindra said, "There she goes." Narayan, nearing the dénouement of the *raag,* ceased playing.

"There goes who?" he asked, dreamily, still in the emotional grip of the melody. The friends conversed in English.

"A whore," answered Rabindra nonchalantly. "My father is one of her clients."

Narayan, intrigued, sat up in an attempt to get a closer look at the boat and its occupants. All he could see was the smudge of a white shape against the dark night, and that too was disappearing.

"Does she look like a whore? She's a widow, you fool," said Narayan, irritated.

"I know she's a widow," replied Rabindra. "The gentry here have an 'unnatural concern' for widows."

GULABI SANG AS SHE ROWED. The muscles on her arms rippled under the short puffed sleeves of her sari blouse. Kalyani was seated on a thinly cushioned bench in front of the boat with her back to Gulabi. She was swaddled in white, and just a sliver of brow and the tip of her nose were visible. The lantern swaying on the prow of the boat illuminated her bowed, sari-covered head. The sweet, plaintive notes of the flute wafted through the night and reached across the river. Gulabi's humming subsided to a faint buzz, and even that faded as she stilled the oars to listen to the flute. Transported by the distant music, Kalyani turned to Gulabi. With dreamy smiles and swaying heads, she and the eunuch shared the melodious moment. Kalyani slowly turned away when the music faded and stared impassively into the dark.

"Gulabi *behen*?" she ventured, interrupting Gulabi's song.

"Hmm?" said the songstress.

"Does Lord Krishna take on human form?"

"Of course he does!" replied Gulabi, in her usual assured and yet unconvincing manner. "Haven't you seen us perform his life story? He plays himself," Gulabi comically batted her kohl-lined eyes and simpered, "while I play his adoring milkmaid."

She tittered at her own joke, and the beginnings of a smile animated Kalyani's face as the irrepressible music-lover broke into song.

But then Kalyani remembered the nature of their nocturnal journey, and her eyes dimmed. Her body stiffened as she prepared herself for the rest of the night—she had learned to retreat to a place deep inside herself where her emotions could not be violated, despite what happened to her body.

"THE FAMILY'S WAITING up for me. We'd better go," Narayan said, getting up from the steps and offering Rabindra a hand.

They made an incongruous pair as they strolled along the *ghats*. Narayan, tall and broad-shouldered, dapper in a homespun *dhoti* and white *kurta*, and Rabindra, a head shorter, decked out in Western clothes ill-suited to his sloping shoulders and protruding paunch. He had large, undefined features, their outline blurred by fat and short brown hair.

Rabindra took a draught of Scotch from his flask

"My father doesn't even bother with their names anymore. There's the old one, the fat one, the new one, the young one..."

"You should get your father to join Gandhi!"

Narayan took firm hold of his friend's hand and, holding it aloft, wickedly announced, "'Seth Bhupindernath and Gandhi, hand in hand, will liberate the widows of India from their plight!'"

Some people loitering along the steps looked their way, but they couldn't follow the English words and lost interest in the drunken behaviour of the two men.

Rabindra stifled a laugh. "Does your father 'concern' himself with widows?" he asked

"No," Narayan replied quickly. "Absolutely not. He would never do such a thing."

"Well, perhaps he should think about becoming a philanthropist," Rabindra said.

Narayan was quiet for a moment. "Doesn't it bother you?"

"What? My father's involvement with the widows? Not at all." He spoke lightly, but something in his tone warned Narayan to back off.

Rabindra tugged roughly at the brown cloth-satchel hanging from Narayan's shoulder. "You've gone totally 'native,' man: *khaddar*-clothes, *jhola*-bags, playing *raags* on *bansaris*."

Narayan remained silent, tapping his flute absent-mindedly.

"What's on your mind?" Rabindra asked.

"Have you ever thought about joining the Congress?"

"Are you crazy? I happen to like English ways: their cricket, their whiskey—and what poets they have! 'She walks like a beauty in the night...,'" he recited, extending an arm and almost stumbling as he tried to swirl.

Narayan held out a steadying hand and corrected: "'She walks in beauty, like the night.' If Gandhi can free India, think how Byron will sound when you recite him as a free man."

They sought out a tree-lined path that led along the *ghats*.

"You haven't become a Nationalist, have you?" Rabindra asked, probing his friend's face in the red and orange light that radiated around them. Dots of red light twinkled through the trees.

Narayan shrugged. "Passive Resistance!" he said. "Think about it. How long can the British fight someone who refuses to fight? Gandhi is a modern-day prophet! A prophet for our times!"

"Forget it," Rabindra advised. "Romantics like you make terrible nationalists." He raised his flask to Narayan. "Here's to Byron and a concern for gorgeous widows."

He took a swig and offered the flask to his friend.

"Here's to Passive Resistance and *bansaris*!" Narayan raised the flask and took a long, thirsty draught.

"Forget about politics. Enjoy life," Rabindra advised, putting an arm around his friend, as they took a path that led away from the river and the *ghats*.

Chapter Eight

≋

Shakuntala stood knee-deep in the water, head bowed, arms extended, offering dawn prayers to the Holy River. Bells in hundreds of temples rang throughout the city to awaken the populace and recall them to worship. A muezzin's cry, fragmented by the breeze, summoned the faithful to prayer. Chuyia hung around, bored, splashing her hands lightly in the water. She was fed up with Shakuntala's constant prayers. Her mother had also worshipped the statues of her favourite gods and goddesses, but she did not instruct her to pray with her each time. Besides, her ma didn't pray so much: she had a family to take care of!

The river, chill and steely grey-green at this hour, was already dotted with people busily washing their clothes and bathing. Leached of colour by the dawn light, everything appeared white. On a white stone wall stood a pristine white statue of a miniature cow with garlands around its neck; as Chuyia idly cast her eyes on it, a real cow sauntered up and placidly stood by it, chewing on its cud. Nearby, a woman soaped her dark skin with white suds. Scraps of grey-white smoke from the *ghat* drifted over them.

"O sacred river, radiant like the moon..." Shakuntala sang in a trained, husky voice.

Chuyia clasped her palms beneath her chin, and chanted, "Radiant like the autumn moon..."

"Home of the Eminent...," continued Shakuntala.

"Re...," Chuyia stopped mid-word and, letting her arms drop to her sides, interrupted Shakuntala. "When do we stop praying?"

Shakuntala silenced Chuyia with a stern look. She splashed water backwards with both hands to complete the interrupted ritual.

They finished bathing, and Chuyia walked behind Shakuntala, wringing out her soaked sari. Shakuntala glanced over her shoulder and noticed Chuyia's drenched clothes.

"Don't you have a dry sari?" she asked.

"It's in *your* house," replied Chuyia, emphasizing the word "your" to let Shakuntala know she still considered herself a temporary guest of the *ashram*, not a permanent resident.

"Bring it tomorrow," instructed Shakuntala

"Tomorrow, I'll be in *my* house," Chuyia stubbornly insisted.

"Fine," Shakuntala said, lengthening her stride, and Chuyia scrambled to keep up with her.

They climbed a short flight of steps and arrived at a clearing skirted by a white stone railing. Sadananda sat under a mushroom-shaped umbrella, reading to his congregation. A heavily built man in his mid-fifties with a kindly, creased face, he wore a *dhoti*, and the sacred thread that lay across his bare chest and bulging belly rose and fell to the calm rhythm of his breathing. The sandal-wood paste on his forehead marked him as a priest.

Sadananda had long ago come to terms with the occupational hazards of ministering to his flock of widows. When he had first assumed his duties as a young priest, he had been overwhelmed by the proximity of their bodies, ripe beneath coarse, loosely-spun saris that stretched to accommodate each curve and dent of their desirable flesh and left little to the imagination. He lusted after the young, the middle-aged and, except for the very old, even the elderly. The widows' saris covered only one shoulder and the hollow in their collarbones made him want to bury his face in their necks. The combination of moral turpitude and innocence with the voluptuous joggle of flesh under the saris gave an unsustainably erotic charge. And the eroticism was heightened by their vulnerability and availability. He had succumbed and occasionally taken advantage of the access his position as their priest and mentor gave him. If the gods lusted and got what they wanted, how was he, a puny mortal, to resist the allure of these women?

Shakuntala and Chuyia took a place in the semicircle of widows squatting around Sadananda in various attitudes of repose and comfort. The white of Chuyia's scalp shone through the dark hair struggling to grow back. The skin of her back and arms, burnt a dark nutty-brown by the sun, was set off by the white sari. The sari was still wet and clung to her untidily.

Their heads respectfully covered, the wizened, despondent-looking women with grim faces and dimmed eyes nodded in affirmation to the priests' measured words. They all wore the dual-pronged ash-marks on their foreheads. A woman they had not seen before, who was about the same age as Shakuntala, sat hunched over, her head resting on her hand as if her neck could no longer bear its burden. Shakuntala noticed the troubled look on Chuyia's face and whispered, "She is new. She'll be all right." Shakuntala didn't know how to comfort this child.

Sadananda read from the Ramayana in a soothing, sonorous voice. He had noticed Shakuntala's arrival with Chuyia. His face creased into a welcoming smile, and he bobbed his head to acknowledge their presence. Looking kindly at the little girl, he remarked, "What have we here...a new widow." He cast his eye on Shakuntala. "It's good you brought her."

Chuyia felt shy in the face of this attention and buried her head in Shakuntala's shoulder.

Shakuntala reprimanded her sharply, "Sit up straight."

Sadananda came to Chuyia's defence. "Don't scold her, she's just a child."

Kunti, sitting nearby, could not help interjecting. "Child, indeed! She's turned the house upside down. I still have bruises from her kicks." Kunti raised her sari to show a bruise on her shin. "Scratch-marks." She pushed back the sari from her shoulder and pointed to a line of scabs.

Muttering and nodding in agreement with Kunti's pronouncement, all the other widows joined their raised voices in condemnation of Chuyia. Snehlata exchanged a conspiratorial look with Kunti. Shakuntala wondered what the child could have done to aggravate them so. She did not blame her for fighting the way she had when she first arrived at the *ashram*. After all, she was a child, and it must have been terrifying for her to be so abruptly separated from family and friends and be plunked in the middle of a bunch of dour old women, all strangers to her.

Sadananda looked around, sizing up the situation. He was accustomed to the widows' sudden outbursts and emotional displays. He knew how few opportunities they had to vent their frustration and express their rage at the hand their karmas had dealt them. Because of his kindness and understanding, he often attracted the brunt of these cathartic outbursts and comforted them with stories from the scriptures and nuggets of wisdom from the sacred books. Sadananda raised his voice markedly and, using it like a tuning instrument, continued with his soothing sing-song recitation. This had the intended effect on the widows. They grew calm once again. Kunti and Snehlata closed their eyes in meditation, and the others moved their heads in rhythm with Sadananda's voice.

Chuyia studied the widows carefully, looking at each in turn. She was clearly puzzled about something. They were all women. Even the lantern-jawed, flat-chested ones whom she had thought were men. She had presumed that the white length of cloth they were wrapped in was a uniform worn by both men and women widows —only the women called them saris. She nudged Shakuntala and, in a voice that carried, innocently asked, "*Didi*, where is the house for the men widows?"

There was a stunned silence. Then pandemonium broke out. A chorus of scolding erupted from the shocked widows: "Good God!" "What a horrible thing to say!" "God protect our men from such a fate!" "May your tongue burn!" "Pull out her tongue and throw it in the river." "I'll do it!" they shrieked like harpies.

Shakuntala watched them in silence. She exchanged a troubled glance with Sadananda and, as Chuyia leaned into her for comfort and protection, Shakuntala's stiff body became as yielding and soft as her mother's.

Sadananda raised his sonorous voice even more and continued reading out from the Ramayana.

LATER IN THE MORNING, after they had returned from the sermon, Kunti sat on a low wooden seat, furtively stuffing her mouth with rice. She was eating from a *thali* laden with *daal*, rice and vegetables intended for Madhumati. Next to her, three discoloured iron pots cooked busily on a clay stove.

"Where has that Kunti gone and died," shouted Madhumati from her room, and then she bellowed, "Kunti, bring my food!"

Mouth still full, Kunti called back, "Coming, *didi*," and hurried off to deliver Madhumati's meal. She returned quickly and took her plate of food to the verandah. The other widows were already sitting cross-legged, silently eating their simple meals. She swept a snotty glance past Chuyia and pointedly sat down with her back to her.

Chuyia was shovelling food into her mouth without pausing to take a breath. She realized that Kalyani had not yet joined them. "*Didi*, where is Kalyani?" she asked Shakuntala.

"You and your questions," Kunti muttered. "She eats up our heads!" she complained to the widows at large.

"Witch!" Chuyia mumbled, loud enough so Kunti could hear.

Kunti turned round and slapped Chuyia. "Shut up! Black-tongue."

None of the women protested. An impertinent child had to be punished, and it was high time this child was slapped.

Chuyia accepted the slap in the spirit in which it was administered and continued to eat.

Old Bua cautioned, "Eat slowly, child. Chew each grain carefully. Your next meal is tomorrow."

Ignoring her advice, Chuyia continued to wolf down her food. Shakuntala rose and went to the well to wash her *thali*.

Now that the punishment had been administered, Kunti decided to address Chuyia's query. "Eating with Kalyani would pollute our food," she said with a snooty edge of malice in her voice.

Snehlata explained, "Her head's not shaven, you see."

While the others continued gossiping, Chuyia carefully folded her banana leaf over the uneaten half of her meal to make a small, neat parcel. She tucked it into her sari, and crossed the courtyard casually toward Kalyani's stairs. Once there, she bounded up to the terrace.

Kalyani was on the terrace doing her washing, absently registering snatches of the widows' conversation that drifted up from below. She smiled as Chuyia appeared at the top of the stairs to deliver the rest of her meal to Kaalu. The puppy bounded up to greet her and licked the banana leaf clean.

They heard Kunti say, "I don't even remember being seven."

Old Bua piped up, "What did she say?"

Snehlata told her wistfully, "She says she doesn't remember being seven."

Bua giggled with delight. "Ask me, I do!" she crowed triumphantly. "I remember! I got married when I was seven."

The other widows remained silent as Bua launched into her favourite story, the detailed description of all the glorious sweets served at her wedding: "I had never seen a display like that before. I didn't even pay attention to my husband, I was so fascinated...plump, juicy *rasgullas*, piping hot *gulab jamuns*, cashew-nut sweets covered with gold leaf, yellow *laddoos* dripping in butter. I ate them all when I was seven...."

∞

NARAYAN GAZED ABSENTLY at the traffic of horse-drawn carriages, bullock-carts and pedestrians on the street outside the tea-stall window. He was at a tea stall near the *ashram*, and this was the third glass of tea he was desultorily stirring. He seemed to arrive at a decision; the proprietor looked at him hopefully. "More tea, sir?"

"No," Narayan shook his head resolutely and, after paying the proprietor at the counter, took off in the direction of Madhumati's *ashram*. He had dressed with care, and he knew he looked well in a starched white *dhoti* with a black suit jacket over his *kurta*, a jaunty orange scarf laid out neatly over one shoulder. When he arrived at the large, forbidding door, his resolve weakened and he hesitated outside the slightly warped panels. He squared his shoulders and knocked politely once. No one answered the door. He tried again, knocking twice and with more firmness.

Shakuntala slid open the small window in the door and peered out. Her eyes widened at the sight of the well-dressed stranger, who stood looking at her nervously.

"What do you want?" she asked brusquely. Handsome young men who turned up at the *ashram* were treated with suspicion.

"Uh...Is Chuyia here?" Narayan said, thinking on his feet, glad he'd had the presence of mind not to ask for Kalyani.

"Are you a relative?"

"A friend," Narayan said.

"Men are not allowed here." Shakuntala shut the door firmly in Narayan's face.

Crestfallen, Narayan trudged off down the alley. Just as he turned a corner, he was startled by a shower of cold water that fell directly onto his head from above. He looked up angrily for the source of this insult, shouting, "Can't you watch what you're doing?"

Kalyani and Chuyia, who together had been wringing out Kalyani's freshly washed sari, peeked over the roof in alarm. Kalyani, recognizing Narayan, was remorseful and at the same time electrified by his presence. Hair plastered to his face, his fine clothes dripping, Narayan stood there like a drowned god.

Narayan stared, transfixed by her beauty, mortified that he had shouted so boorishly.

"Please forgive us," Kalyani apologized demurely.

"No—it's all right," Narayan said, stammering and grinning, almost falling over his two soggy left feet. "You can do it again if you want," he added gallantly.

Narayan, feeling he was making a fool of himself, quit talking and stared up at Kalyani. She gave him a fleeting, shy smile and, sinking behind the roof wall, disappeared from view.

"Where is she?" Narayan asked Chuyia, speaking in a courtly manner.

"She's hiding," answered Chuyia matter-of-factly. The turn of events delighted her.

"Will she come out?"

Chuyia turned for a moment and then pronounced, "No."

Narayan remained standing awkwardly on the street, still hoping Kalyani would materialize above the parapet. After a few minutes, he nodded and started to walk away, but he had taken barely five steps when he turned and called, "Please give her a message for me. Tell her I liked it when she spilled the water on me!"

"Did you hear that?" Chuyia asked.

Kalyani's radiant eyes and smiling face answered for her.

"He's gone!" Chuyia reported.

Kalyani rose to her knees to peer over the parapet, and her eyes clung to Narayan's broad, retreating back. They both craned their necks, hoping he would turn to look at them, but Narayan had willed himself not to do so.

Chapter Nine

✄

Thunder rumbled in the distance. Lightning zigzagged through the sooty bank of clouds approaching from the horizon, and, preceded by the fecund scent of water on parched earth, the monsoon season stormed into Rawalpur. The dark skies unleashed a torrent of rain, and one by one the widows emerged from various recesses of the *ashram* and turned their ravaged faces to the rain. Chuyia raced up the stairs to Kalyani and excitedly pulled her to the terrace, but Kalyani retreated to the shelter of the doorway and stood there, shivering. Chuyia splashed beneath the streams of water cascading off the roof and, Kaalu, who had been cowering under Kalyani's cot, cautiously came out and stood besides his mistress. He sniffed and gingerly stepped onto the wet and, with a cowardly yelp, shied back when the enormous drops of rain pelted him. Laughing at him, Kalyani stepped out into the rain and, spreading her arms, rotated slowly. She reached her hands out to Chuyia and, clasping each other's crossed hands, faces uplifted to the onslaught of water and wind, they whirled faster and faster as Kaalu ran around them barking excitedly. Nearly losing their balance with giddiness, they fell, laughing against each other, and held on fast as the terrace undulated in a crazy dance beneath their feet.

All afternoon the widows celebrated the arrival of the rainy season, clapping hands and singing songs remembered from childhood to welcome rain, and on the terrace Kalyani's new love burgeoned within her with giddy abandon.

The rain caught Narayan on his way to the bookstore, and the heavy monsoon downpour soaked him through to his skin. He recalled at once the other time he'd been rained upon, and Kalyani's apologetic face as it peeped over the roof to say, "Please forgive us." He extended his arms reverently to the rain and joyously shouted at the sky, "It's all right! You can do it again if you want!" The wind tore his umbrella from his grasp and sent it floating and rolling down the street ahead of him and, laughing, he ran after it. The lashing monsoon storm harmonized with the tumultuous passions spinning within him, and graced him with an exhilarating sense of invincibility. His joy quickened his stride, broadened his smile, and he burst into his home soaking wet, smiling stupidly. He was smitten—in love with Kalyani! He wanted to shout it to the world.

≋

THE ONSET OF THE MONSOON changed the rhythm of Chuyia's life. Cooped up in the *ashram*, time hung heavy on her hands and she sought friends among the widows. She pestered Kunti to play hopscotch with her. Kunti brushed her away, scolding, "Have I nothing better to do than play with spoiled brats?" But Kunti, young enough to recall the wonderful games she had played with her friends in their tribal village, relented. They drew squares on the verandah and, throwing broken tiles into the squares, they played *ganga-jamuna*, leaping from square to square, while the rain pelted the courtyard and the widows, for want of anything to do, sat on their haunches against the walls and watched. Chuyia persuaded Kalyani to come downstairs, and Kunti joined them in a game of hide-and-seek. They crouched in corners while the widows pretended not to see them, and the young women yelped in delight when they found each other.

Chuyia spent the mornings playing with Kaalu. Everyone knew about Kaalu's secret existence—how could they not—but pretended not to. With the run of the terrace and the privacy she enjoyed, her uncut hair and Kaalu, Kalyani had a privileged position. Chuyia accepted this, as she accepted Shakuntala's independent authority, and if she sometimes wondered about it, she never dwelt on it. Some of the widows, like Kunti, resented Kalyani, but Madhumati was considerate of her welfare. Kalyani avoided Madhumati, Chuyia suspected, but on the few occasions she had seen them together Madhumati talked to her with a special sweetness.

One afternoon, a week into the monsoon, when the rain had turned the courtyard into a shallow lake and the overflow flooded parts of the surrounding verandah, Chuyia wandered listlessly into Shakuntala's room. Shakuntala was reading. Chuyia leaned against the wall and, restlessly kicking it with her heel, complained, "It will never stop raining."

Shakuntala turned around and looked at Chuyia in her thoughtful way. "Well, maybe you can take this time to learn something for once. Come—I'll read to you."

Chuyia plunked down on the floor next to her. She glanced at the cover of the book. "The Mahabharata!" she exclaimed. "My ma told me stories from that book."

"You can read?" Shakuntala asked, surprised.

"*Amma* taught me some words," she said proudly. "I know that word. My brothers taught me the alphabet."

Shakuntala understood what she meant: she could recognize a few whole words by the shapes they made.

"Would you like to learn more words? I can teach you," she said.

Chuyia sidled up to her and nodded shyly. "What will you read to me?"

"Did your mother tell you the story of Shakuntala?"

"No," Chuyia said. She paused. "Is the story in the Mahabharata?"

"Yes, it is."

Chuyia twisted her neck to look directly at her. "Are you named after the Shakuntala in the book?"

"No," Shakuntala responded gravely. "She's named after me."

"Oh!" Chuyia's eyes and mouth grew round, and she very nearly believed her, until she glimpsed a twitch in the corner of Shakuntala's mouth. "That's not true!" she cried, rolling away from her, embarrassed at being fooled and at the same time delighted by the teasing. It was the kind of joke her brothers played on her. She looked at

Shakuntala with renewed interest, surprised by this unexpected facet of her nature.

"Come," Shakuntala said, smiling as she extended a hand. "I'll tell you the story."

Chuyia sat attentively, as Shakuntala read the title of the story, "'Dushyanta and Shakuntala.'" As she read the story, her voice acquired the spellbinding rhythm and lilt Chuyia's mother's voice had acquired when she read from the religious texts.

"Shakuntala was given by her father to the sage Kanva, head of a forest *ashram*. The sage loved her like a daughter, and Shakuntala grew up to become a most beautiful and modest woman. Her voice was sweet, and her manners sober and gracious."

"Why did her father give her away to the sage?" Chuyia asked, not happy with this bit of news.

"Sometimes fathers have to give their daughters away," Shakuntala said gently.

"They shouldn't!" Chuyia said, looking at the floor to hide the sudden tears that sprang to her eyes.

"Do you want to hear the story or not?" Shakuntala asked, pretending she hadn't noticed Chuyia's distress.

Chuyia nodded and mumbled, "Yes."

Shakuntala continued.

"One day, the great King Dushyanta happened to come near the *ashram* while he was out hunting. He caught sight of Shakuntala, and lost his heart to her beauty and grace. The king proposed to Shakuntala, and they were married secretly. Dushyanta stayed overnight, but he had to leave for his kingdom; he promised Shakuntala that he would send for her. The king gave her his most precious ring, and told Shakuntala that she must never lose it.

"As fate would have it, King Dushyanta became so occupied with ruling his kingdom that he forgot all about Shakuntala."

"Like you," Chuyia said, getting her own back. "Everyone has forgotten you!"

Shakuntala was so taken aback, she didn't know what to say.

"Why do you say that?" she asked quietly.

"Isn't it true?" Chuyia said.

There was a pause during which Shakuntala shut her eyes. "What you say is true," she said at last, her voice so meek and resigned that it shamed Chuyia.

Chuyia edged up to her, rubbing her cheek on Shakuntala's arm and raised her eyes to her face. "You are my Durga," she said by way of apology. After a moment of silence, she said, "Then what happened?"

"Then what," Shakuntala said. "You'll interrupt again."

Chuyia looked contrite enough to appease Shakuntala, so she began to read again.

"Shakuntala became very worried when her husband did not send for her. The worry turned into panic when she discovered she was pregnant. Sage Kanva decided to send her to her husband's kingdom, where she would be accepted as his queen.

"Shakuntala was dressed in beautiful silken clothes, and she left for Dushyanta's kingdom by ferry. The balmy sea breeze soon lulled her, and she fell sleep. The royal ring slipped from her finger into the ocean and was swallowed by a fish. Shakuntala did not even realize she had lost the ring.

"Shakuntala reached the court of Dushyanta, and a message was sent to the king of the arrival of 'a woman who claimed to be his wife.' But Dushyanta had lost his memory of Shakuntala and of their marriage. He refused to accept Shakuntala as his wife. When Shakuntala tried to show him the ring on her finger, she discovered that it was no longer there and she was forced to return home."

Shakuntala placed a silk bookmark at the page. "That's enough for today," she said and closed the book. The expression on Chuyia's face remained rapt.

"Did the king ever remember Shakuntala?" she asked.

"You can find out the next time I read."

"Will you read later?" Chuyia asked.

"Come at about the same time tomorrow afternoon," Shakuntala said. "If it's raining, I will read the rest."

After the initial storming and lashing onslaught that preceded it like a cosmic circus, the monsoon had settled down to a steady downpour with no other purpose than to drain the burden of the clouds piled on top.

It rained all night. It let up for a couple of hours in the morning, and then it poured.

Chuyia presented herself at the appointed time. Shakuntala looked at her steadily, pleased to see her. "Ready?" she asked, and Chuyia scuttled down to the floor and sat down beside her.

Shakuntala opened the book and picked up the story where she had left off.

"Dejected and disappointed, Shakuntala told Sage Kanva she had decided to go to the forest. Sage Kanva gave her his blessings, and Shakuntala went to live in the forest all alone. In due course, she gave birth to a most beautiful and healthy son. She named him Bharata. Bharata grew up in the jungle without any human companions other than his mother. So he spent a great deal of time in the forest, and he became fascinated with the plants, trees and wild animals he found in the jungle. He gradually made friends with all the wild animals, and even the lions and tigers became his friends. They let him ride on their backs like we ride horses."

"He rode the lions and tigers?" Chuyia interrupted, her eyes shining.

"Yes," Shakuntala said. "He was fearless. The mother taught him all the things a young prince should be taught. He became skilled in archery and the use of other weapons. His mother also schooled him in the Scriptures: the Vedas and the Upanishads.

"Bharata grew into a handsome, intelligent and brave youth—a prince in exile!

"Then one day, in the kingdom of Dushyanta, a fisherman caught the fish that had swallowed the royal ring that had slipped from Shakuntala's finger. When he cut open the fish to cook it, he found the ring. The fisherman rushed to the royal court and told the king how he had found the royal ring. When he saw his ring, King Dushyanta remembered everything. He remembered he had fallen in love with the beautiful Shakuntala and had married her. He was very repentant that he had sent his pregnant wife away so heartlessly.

He sent his men to search for Shakuntala all over his kingdom.

"At last, his Minister gave him the good news. He bowed before him and told him that the king's search party had found Shakuntala and her handsome son. They were both safe in the heart of the forest. The king went to fetch his wife and son. He begged their forgiveness, and with due honour and festivity brought them back to the palace and made Shakuntala his queen.

"Years later, when King Dushyanta died, Bharata became the king of ancient India. He was a noble and just king. There was no poverty or misery in his kingdom. That is why India is also known as *Bharatavarsha*—the Land of Bharata."

Shakuntala let the book remain open. Chuyia had edged closer and closer to her as she read the story, until their shoulders were rubbing. When Chuyia glanced up, she found Shakuntala's serious, candid eyes fixed on her.

"The little boy found joy even though he grew up in a jungle with no one to play with, no family except his mother. He became strong and powerful. Perhaps you can learn from him."

"But he was a prince; he got to rule a kingdom," Chuyia said. "And at least he had his mother."

"How do you know you're not a princess?" Shakuntala said.

Chuyia looked at her, startled. There was that hint of a smile. Chuyia shyly snuggled up to her, and Shakuntala felt an unaccustomed tenderness seep through her body. She placed a tentative arm around the child.

SHAKUNTALA WENT TO THE RIVER to get holy water for the priest, Sadananda. As she came to the white stone river enclosure, which was her usual place for filling his ceremonial brass pot, she was charmed by a lovely young bride at the centre of a wedding ceremony. The priest conducting the ceremony was busy anointing a plaster cow draped in an orange sari in front of the bride and groom. Shakuntala knew she should leave and go elsewhere to get the water, but something drew her toward the group. Perhaps it was the desire to witness the joy that radiated from the bride; perhaps it was just a wish to be among happy people. Shakuntala slowly descended the steps. The priest had his back to her, but some members of the wedding party began to stir uneasily. As she stooped to fill the pot with water, the ceremony came to an abrupt halt.

The priest spoke sharply to Shakuntala. "Watch it! Don't let your shadow touch the bride."

Shakuntala stood rooted to the step, in shock at being addressed this way by a priest. Lowering her eyes in apology, she turned her back on the group and ascended the steps with as much dignity as she could muster.

When she handed the brass pot to Sadananda, from the way he lowered his gaze she knew he'd witnessed her humiliation. "Such ignorance," he said softly, taking the pot from her arms. "This ignorance is our misfortune."

Head covered, eyes downcast, Shakuntala did not respond as she prepared the spot for worship—unrolling and smoothing down Sadananda's straw mat and sprinkling holy water. Sadananda gazed at her with unmistakable gratitude and affection. He placed a hand cautiously on her shoulder. "Shakuntala-*devi*, you've been doing this for so many years."

When she didn't respond, he sighed, spreading out the Ramayana, incense, sandalwood paste and holy water. He continued, "So many years of service and devotion. Do you feel any closer to self-liberation?"

Shakuntala did not answer immediately. She said, "If self-liberation means detachment from worldly desires, then no, I'm no closer to it."

He let his hand rest for a moment on her shoulder. "Whatever happens," he said, his voice weighted with concern, "never lose your faith."

Shakuntala looked at Sadananda thoughtfully. He was a good man: she trusted him.

Chapter Ten

꠸

The widows formed a long, snaking line as they sat outside the temple in their white saris with their begging bowls. The evening sun was behind them, and it cast a mellow glow on the rain-washed temple and the trees bursting with leaves. They had grown as accustomed to begging as they had to the gruelling hours of singing in temple halls to earn a few coins and a fistful of rice. Without these handouts, they would starve. They had long ago lost their initial sense of shame and humiliation at accepting alms. The irony was that most of the widows, from villages in Bengal and neighbouring Bihar were from landowning families and were in fact accustomed to giving alms to the less fortunate. But that was long ago.

Chuyia sat between Shakuntala and Snehlata with only a vague idea of why they were there. Shakuntala had told her that it was the evening of the Durga Festival, and people were inclined to be generous. The *ashram* barber, a slight nervous man with buckteeth, had arrived the day before with his razor and shaved all their heads to a smooth baldness in preparation for the festival.

A woman and her daughter came out of the temple. The young girl, no older than seven, wore her brilliant red skirt and blouse proudly. A chain of white jasmine-buds adorned her long hair, and her hands were covered in bangles. Her mother handed the girl a coin. Chuyia locked eyes with her; the girl's gaze was friendly.

The girl stood looking at Chuyia solemnly for a moment, and then gave her the coin. Chuyia felt the blood rise to her face, and her humiliation was like a blow that winded her. She clenched the coin tightly in her fist to contain her fury. Shakuntala gave her a stern look; she should have thanked the girl. The mother was handing out coins to the other widows down the line.

The young girl walking away with her mother shook her wrists to hear the jingle of her bangles. Although she had few recollections of her wedding, Chuyia suddenly remembered her red sari, the glittering gold pendant hanging on her forehead, the red and green bangles jangling on her wrists. As soon as the mother and daughter were gone from view, Chuyia turned to Shakuntala and hissed, "I hate you!"

She leapt up and ran away.

The widow sitting next to Shakuntala leaned over her to observe, "She's still not used to this."

"It's her first time," Shakuntala said coldly. "She'll get used to it. We all do."

⋙⋘

THE TUMULT OF CHUYIA'S emotions carried her through the streets randomly until she arrived at a lane

118

filled with the aromas of all the fried foods forbidden to her, and her rage was banished by the delightful fragrance wafting up her nose. She became aware of the coin biting into her hand, and she loosened her grip on it.

Chuyia stood in front of a vendor, watching wide-eyed as *puris* puffed up like little balloons on a lake of hot oil in a *karahi*.

"Get away!" the vendor shooed Chuyia, as if she were a stray animal.

Chuyia shot back, "I have money."

She held out the small coin in proof.

"Widows don't eat fried food," he said, spitting betel juice into a bowl.

Chuyia stuck her tongue out at him.

The vendor laughed—she was just a kid. "What do you want? Speak up."

Chuyia reluctantly pulled her eyes away from the mouth-watering *puris* and pointed to the only treat she could possibly choose. She placed the coin on the platform on which he sat and, situating herself away from the counter, held out her sari. The man leaned forward and dropped the small packet into it.

IT WAS DARK BY THE TIME Chuyia returned to the *ashram* and timidly knocked on the outside door. Shakuntala opened the top panel, hoping it was her. "Where were you? Is this a time to come back?" she scolded *sotto voce*, as she unlatched the door. "Can't you see how dark it is? Where have you been?" she asked again, but Chuyia was already walking down the passage.

"I'm talking to you. Come here!" Shakuntala said. No one disobeyed her when she used that tone of voice. Chuyia retraced her steps and stood before her. "You can't go running off just because you're upset! Anything could happen to a young girl like you."

Chuyia looked at her meekly. "I won't do it again." She wanted to get on with what she had in mind to do; this should end quickly.

"Madhumati-*didi* asked for you. I pretended I knew where you were. If she'd found out, who knows what she'd do! She would have locked you out."

Hands hanging humbly by her side, Chuyia made an effort to look even more contrite. "Shakuntala-*didi*, I won't do it again."

"I've saved some food for you. Go, eat. But first see what Madhumati-*didi* wants."

Chuyia was anxious to get to Bua, but she obediently went to Madhumati's room. She was relieved to find that Madhumati was occupied with her bath. The bathing cubicle had no door, and Chuyia glimpsed her emptying jugs of water over her rolls of flesh. Madhumati modestly bathed in her sari, as did all the widows. It allowed access to whoever wished to use the space, and it got the saris cleaned as well.

Chuyia stealthily crept to Shakuntala's room. It was past Bua's bedtime and, as Chuyia expected, she lay turned over on her side, snoring and snorting. The loose skin on her hollow cheeks fluttered with each breath, and her lips made small puttering sounds when she breathed out.

Chuyia knelt by the old woman and, holding out the glistening yellow *laddoo*, waved it near her nose. She said softly, "Auntie! Auntie!" a few times to rouse her, and, when she stirred, Chuyia quickly set the *laddoo* on the mat and slipped out of the room. She stayed just outside the doorway to watch Bua's reaction.

Bua's rheumy, scrunched-up eyes widened in astonishment; two inches from her eyeballs sat the most scrumptious yellow *laddoo* in the world! Her eyes glued to the orb of sweet lentil-fudge, she sat up. She was not sure if she was still dreaming, or if this unexpected treasure was for real. She lifted the *laddoo* gingerly, half-expecting it to vanish. It stayed firm and substantial between her fingers. She brought it to her nose and inhaled its fragrance: it was made in pure butter-oil. Then she quickly shoved the whole *laddoo* into her toothless mouth, and with her hand clamped her mouth shut.

The gob of fudge stuffed her mouth so she could scarcely breathe. As the glorious buttery sweetness from it swamped her taste buds, waves of delight spread through her whole body and sent Bua reeling back into her past. Memories shaped themselves into images and scenes that transported her back across the span of years to her wedding day.

Her round face prettied with makeup, her ears, nose, forehead and hair adorned with gold jewellery, she sits beneath the marriage canopy like a beautiful little goddess. The *pandal* is staked out by four sturdy banana stalks, one in each corner, and corralled on three sides by strings of red roses, white jasmine and other flowers, interspersed with fringes of fresh ferns and large tropical leaves. She sits on the stage, which is festooned with coils of gold and silver tinsel, fluffed out in a richly embossed, red-and-gold brocade sari with a wide beaded fringe. Her neck and chest are circled by chains of gold and heavy garlands of rose and jasmine. And right through the wedding ceremony and the celebrations that follow, she feasts her eyes on the sumptuous array of sweets and then finally stuffs her mouth full of them.

The *laddoo* given to Bua by Chuyia, still filling her clamped mouth to capacity, radiated such sweetness that Bua's memories shifted to her mother, as she held Bua tenderly in her arms, whispered gentle instructions she couldn't follow in her ear and affectionately pinched her cheek. The lovely little bride lifted her arms to place the garland from her own neck around the neck of her handsome groom, a man older than her by eight or nine years.

As Bua slowly masticated the flesh of the *laddoo* with her hard gums and little by little, like a boa constrictor, squeezed it down her gullet, she relived the best years of her life: her acceptance by her prosperous new landowning Brahmin family and her happy immersion in their daily routine; the kindness of her gentle mother-in-law who once remarked, "You are our little Lakshmi"; the increasingly comforting embrace of the man she never, even in her thoughts, could name. Her face looked as if she'd attained nirvana.

Chuyia blinked, gratified by the salutary effect her gift had on her friend. She wanted to stay, hear Auntie narrate the stories she was obviously reliving, express her satisfaction at the savour of the longed-for sweet. But Madhumati was calling for her, and, without revealing her presence to Auntie, Chuyia slipped away.

Chapter Eleven

※

Madhumati lay on her stomach like a sedated whale, and her arms lay against her body like limp flippers. Chuyia, holding onto a bar stretched above the bed for balance, stood on the cushion of Madhumati's wide buttocks, shifting her weight from one foot to the other to pummel and massage the obese bottom. Madhumati moaned with pleasure. Heralded by the buzz and hum of her song, Gulabi arrived at the barred window opening on the alley, prepared to share the morning's gossip and while away the time. Mitthu the parrot swung in his cage, repeating with infuriating insistence, "Pretty Madhu! Pretty Madhu!"

Madhumati praised Chuyia's efforts, "Well done, my little mouse! Now do my legs."

Chuyia obliged: hopping down she knelt by Madhumati's bed and began kneading and massaging her flaccid calves with her strong little hands.

"Gently!" cautioned Madhumati, slightly raising her head to look at Chuyia. "My skin is sensitive." Then, to the world at large, which at that point consisted only of Chuyia and Gulabi, she declared, "Even if a mosquito sits

123

on me, it creates a crater." She sighed exaggeratedly and gave Chuyia a fey look. Getting into the spirit of the sport, Gulabi flipped a dainty wrist and cooed, "*Hai*, you poor thing."

Chuyia grinned and continued to work silently. After a while, Madhumati, pummelled to a state of comatose bliss, mumbled, "Ask Gulabi. I always keep my promises. If I say I will do something, I always do it."

"That she does," Gulabi unctuously confirmed, and advanced the conversation to the next level.

"If she says she'll send you home, then she will."

Hope welled in Chuyia's heart, and her eyes lit up. No matter how often Madhumati mumbled these words in her sedated state or how often Gulabi attested to them, Chuyia knew they were barren assertions; yet she could no more tamp the hope that flared in her heart each time she heard them than she could stop breathing. She kneaded Madhumati's thighs with renewed vigour and her little body rocked with the effort. Madhumati shut her eyes in pleasure, and Gulabi took this as a signal to start gossiping.

"Do you know…" she began.

"Know what?" said Madhumati.

"This Gandhi is going to sink India."

"What's he done now?"

"Gandhi says, 'The untouchables are the children of God!'" Gulabi said in a shocked, pious voice.

This news had the desired effect. Madhumati reared up like a scandalized cobra, and shook her head in disbelief. "Disgusting! Before he came, everything ran like an English clock. Tick tock!"

Gulabi chimed in with Madhumati's ticking clock, "Tick tock!" and clapped her hands in a manner typical of eunuchs.

Madhumati appeared to become thoughtful, and a sly look crept into her eyes. "Next he'll be saying, '*Hijras* are the children of God!'"

Gulabi stopped laughing. Then she said, "If untouchables are 'children of God,' then eunuchs are His step-children! Even our earthly mother–father have no claim on us."

Chuyia looked at her round-eyed. "You have mother–father?"

"Everybody has mother–father," Gulabi said. "But when a eunuch is born, whether it is in a palace or hovel, the *hijras* claim it and carry the baby off. The mother–father never see the baby again."

"They carried you off?" Chuyia asked incredulous. "Didn't your mother cry?"

"She must have," Gulabi said indifferently. "All mothers cry when we take their babies."

Hijras were akin to a force of nature even in their villages. When a son was born, within minutes they descended on the house, clapping and raucously singing until their demands were met and they were paid off. But this was the first Chuyia had heard about them carrying babies off.

"How did they know you were a *hijra*?"

"They always know. The very minute a eunuch is born, they know."

"How can they tell a baby is a *hijra*?" Chuyia asked.

"They are half-girl, half-boy."

"You are half-girl, half-boy?"

"Yes. You want to see?" Gulabi said, obligingly unwrapping part of her sari, as Chuyia eagerly crossed the room to the window.

Madhumati's aspect was a study in astonishment as she sat up in bed. "Have you gone raving mad? I'll puke if you show your wretched privates!"

"Who cares what you think," said Gulabi with an affected shrug. "I have enough admirers." She threw her sari *palu* back over her shoulder.

"Shameless madwoman!"

Madhumati turned to Chuyia and irritably snapped, "No more questions. Go and play outside. I've got a headache."

Chuyia tottered out of the room utterly bemused. She still had many questions.

Madhumati turned toward the barred window. "Have you brought the stuff?"

Gulabi foraged sulkily in her pouch and, without deigning to even look at Madhumati, disdainfully held out the pouch as if it were a dead rat.

"It had better be good. The last lot made me sick and cranky."

꙳

CLEARLY SETH BHUPINDERNATH's mansion had seen better days. Chipped busts of Englishmen filled every recessed nook, and the dusty bric-a-brac crowded on tables and mantels gave it a cluttered look.

Rabindra and Narayan were in one of the mansion's cavernous living rooms. Rabindra sang a *lied* from

Schubert's *Die schöne Müllerin* with lusty abandon and accompanied himself on a baby grand piano. A glass of red wine stood on top of the piano.

Narayan sat on a divan, absently gazing at a crystal chandelier, its lustre dimmed by neglect; occasionally, when Rabindra took liberties with the aria and his singing set his teeth on edge, he glanced at the chunky figure at the piano and grimaced.

Outside the mansion, Gulabi sashayed down the familiar length of the verandah with a forward thrust of her swaying hips, the silver rings gleaming dully on her dusty toes. She turned to glance at Kalyani; her covered head bowed, hands clasped tight to her sari, Kalyani shuffled several feet behind her. As they walked past the stately columns that supported the verandah, Rabindra's rich tenor drifted out the French doors of the living room. A bored servant, slouching on the floor and leaning against a pillar, held out his hand as they passed. With a coquettish shake of her shoulder and a grimace, Gulabi dropped a coin into his hand. Without bothering to glance at them, the servant slipped the coin into a fold of his turban. Gulabi looked back to make sure Kalyani was following.

They arrived at a spiral staircase made out of rusting metal. It was the servant's staircase. Gulabi started up, but Kalyani hesitated at the foot of the stairs and looked back to the French windows from which came the sound of the singing.

Gulabi turned and hissed, "You'll be seen."

"Take me back," Kalyani replied with uncharacteristic firmness. "I don't want to go up—"

Gulabi's eyes grew wide in alarm. "Are you insane?"

"I want to go back," Kalyani insisted.

"Then you tell that to the client yourself!" Gulabi grabbed Kalyani firmly by both wrists and all but hoisted her up the stairs. Kalyani was shocked by the steely strength in those swarthy arms.

The singing grated on Narayan's ears, and he finally walked across the room and clapped a hand over Rabindra's mouth. His friend's plump face felt too soft. Narayan leaned on the piano and smiled into Rabindra's startled, bloodshot eyes.

"To interrupt someone in the middle of a recital is an insult, Narayan."

Rabindra, offended, shut the piano with an air of injury and crossed the room to a large window.

Narayan smiled, saying, "You can do the same when I sing." He walked over to placate his friend. He glanced out of the window and caught sight of Gulabi perched like some large nightmarish parakeet on the balcony rail of a second-floor room.

"Who's that?" Narayan asked.

"A eunuch, my father's pimp. In *proper* English, a procurer," Rabindra answered nonchalantly.

Narayan looked pained by this answer. Rabindra shrugged and said, "There's a famous saying... 'Widows, bulls, slippery steps and holy men. Avoid these, and Enlightenment awaits.'"

There was no overt reaction from Narayan. Rabindra left his pensive friend at the window and crossed the room to drape a doily over his head; in imitation of a lovestruck Juliet, he recited in falsetto, "'Romeo, oh Romeo, wherefore art thou, Romeo?'"

Narayan, exasperated, said, "Can't you ever be serious?"

Rabindra shrugged his shoulders and gave up his Juliet gig. He retrieved his wine and reclined on a chaise.

Narayan began to lecture Rabindra. "Say you had a wife..."

"I'm not married," interrupted Rabindra.

"Just imagine you were...and she died. And everything you've cared for is taken away from you."

"If you hadn't met that widow, you wouldn't be such a champion of their cause," Rabindra interrupted acidly.

Narayan was miserable. "I don't even know how to see her again."

Rabindra, still refusing to acknowledge the strength of Narayan's feelings for Kalyani, quipped, "Stand beneath her balcony and quote Romeo. People here don't know Shakespeare."

"You disgust me. You really are a Brown Englishman! I'll tell you one thing, Rabindra, your precious English are not going to last!" Narayan was almost shouting.

"And who's going to take their place? Your Gandhi?" said Rabindra sarcastically.

"Of course," answered Narayan with conviction.

The friends sat in strained, unexpectedly hostile silence, and, after a few desultory attempts at polite conversation, Narayan stood up. "It's quite late, I'd better go home."

Getting up to ring the bell, Rabindra said, "I'll tell them to bring the carriage."

"Don't," Narayan said. "I prefer to walk."

Chapter Twelve

✖

Shakuntala's eyes snapped open. She sat up, alarmed by the sounds of choking and laboured breathing. There was something wrong with Bua. Shakuntala lit the oil lamp and quickly went over to her. The old widow lay on her side, curled up like a shrivelled river-shrimp, writhing and gasping for air and moaning. Chuyia lay fast asleep on her mat alongside Bua's. Shakuntala crouched next to Bua and felt for her pulse. A frown deepened the creases on her brow when she felt how thready it was. She sat down on the floor. Leaning close to Bua, stroking her arm, she spoke to her gently in her husky voice. "You'll be all right. Don't worry; I'm here," she said reassuringly. She wiped beads of sweat off the skeletal brow, troubled by how quickly they formed again.

"Take me outside. Take me outside." Bua fretted and, speaking between her rasping breaths and moans, she said, "I want another *laddoo. Hai Ram,* I want a *laddoo.*"

Despite the gravity of the situation, Shakuntala could not help but smile. Just then, Kalyani, who had heard the groans and rushed down the stairs, appeared at the

131

doorway. She stood quietly, taking in the situation, ready to help however she could.

Shakuntala murmured, "Try to sleep." Then, as an afterthought, she asked her, "Do you want water?"

"I want to die in the open," was Bua's heart-wrenching reply.

"No!" Shakuntala gasped. With each passing moment she was becoming increasingly aware of how much Bua meant to her. Who else did she have? She bent her head to Bua's chest, listening for her heartbeat.

Kalyani, sensing time was short for Bua, intervened, saying calmly but firmly, "*Didi*, we should take her outside."

As they gently lifted the frail old woman and between them carried her out into the courtyard, they were shocked at how light she was. "Kalyani, lay out the mat. I'll hold her," Shakuntala instructed, taking Bua into her arms. Bua, who had become quiet, hooked a skinny arm around Shakuntala's neck. Kalyani quickly spread the mat in the courtyard, and between them they gently laid her on it.

Kalyani went in to fetch Bua's thin, board-like pillow. She knelt beside Chuyia and, stroking her head, awakened her. "Chuyia, Bua is not well," Kalyani said. Chuyia noticed the empty space where Bua's mat should be; she gave a cry.

"It's all right. She's outside. Come, let's go."

Kalyani hastily rearranged her sari as Chuyia impatiently pulled away and ran out into the courtyard.

The clay lamp burning beside Bua cast wavering shadows on her shrivelled face. Shakuntala sat leaning over her, as if sheltering her with her body, and held her hand tightly in hers. Chuyia and Kalyani sat on the verandah steps, huddled close. News had a way of travelling swiftly in the *ashram*, and one by one the widows came out from their various recesses to keep vigil; even Madhumati sat at watch.

A hint of dawn began to dilute the night. A stray dog barked, and other dogs joined their desultory barking with his. A cock crowed in the distance. Madhumati sat on a chair Kunti had brought out for her; her *takth* was too far. She sighed dramatically and took charge. "Bua is so lucky," she said, gazing indulgently at the dying woman and spreading her arms at the wonder of it. "Brahmin widows keeping a vigil. For free!"

Snehlata shot her a dirty look, but the other widows ignored her customary coarseness. Shakuntala continuously whispered God's name into Bua's ear, "Ram, Ram, Ram…"

After a long period of silence, during which a few widows went into the house to relieve themselves and hurried back to their vigil, Bua muttered, "Shakuntala! Holy water!"

Shakuntala quickly turned to Chuyia and ordered, "Get some water from the river. Hurry!"

Chuyia nodded solemnly, gratefully accepting the responsibility for carrying out this task for her beloved friend. She grabbed the steel pot that sat on the rim of the well and rushed out the doors of the *ashram*.

As Chuyia hurried in the direction of the river, running part of the way, the air grew lighter and the sky paled. She passed small white temples, white goats, white statues of cows, men praying in the white dawn. She descended the stone steps leading down to the river and quickly filled the pot. Holding the pot in both hands, careful not to spill the water, she hurried back the way she had come. When she turned into the alley leading to the *ashram*, she was stopped by a voice she at once recognized. It was Narayan.

"Chuyia! Remember me—Narayan?" He sat in a cradle formed by the roots of an ancient tree, leaning against its vast trunk, holding the book he was presumably reading in his hand. Chuyia wondered at his vigilance; he had known the instant she arrived in the alley and had called her name. Chuyia turned toward him and nodded "yes."

With a slight toss of his head toward the *ashram*, Narayan sheepishly asked, "Is Kalyani inside?"

"Yes," Chuyia replied. But, intent on her errand, she started to walk away. Looking back over her shoulder, she explained, "I have to go."

"Wait!" Narayan pleaded, calling her back. "Just a minute," he said. Chuyia reluctantly came toward him. Quickly, he tore a page from his book, scribbled a note in Hindi, folded it small and then knelt in front of Chuyia so that he was looking up into her eyes and beseeched her, "Please take this to Kalyani?"

For the second time in the span of one short morning, Chuyia accepted the responsibility of serving a friend. She brought her head forward in answer to his request and handed him the pot of water to free her hands. She took the note from Narayan and tucked it carefully into the waist of her sari. Then, taking back the pot, she walked purposefully off around the corner, water spilling from the pot as she went.

Back at the ashram, Chuyia stood at the top of the stairs leading down to the courtyard, taking in the scene. Bua's small form was wrapped in a white sheet and circled by a thick, shifting band of widows. She was lying on her back, eyes shut, her toothless mouth closed in a restful smile and covered with a tulsi leaf, silent and still. The widows were weeping, heads bowed. Madhumati sat in her chair indifferently fanning herself.

"*Didi*, I've brought water," Chuyia called to Shakuntala.

Shakuntala turned slowly to meet her eyes. "You're too late," she said, her voice heavy with weariness and grief.

Chuyia, dismayed, dropped the pot. It banged and splashed, as it bounced down the stairs. Chuyia turned and ran out of the *ashram*.

"Chuyia!" Kalyani called after her.

Shakuntala started to rise, but was stopped by Kunti who, turning to Madhumati, said coldly, "The money for the cremation?"

There was complete silence.

The widows turned and looked expectantly at Madhumati. She was ready with her excuses. "Every penny from Kalyani's work goes to pay the rent."

Turning to Kunti, she ordered, "Go get Bua's things."

Kunti hurried inside and quickly returned with a little bundle of ragged cloth, a begging bowl, a walking stick and a tattered grass mat. She crouched before it, opened the bundle and set it at Madhumati's feet.

Madhumati irreverently pawed through the contents with her big toe. There was an old sari and a tin box containing Bua's sandalwood paste. "Nothing," she pronounced, and shoved the bundle aside with her foot. The other widows immediately scrambled forward to fight for whatever they could grasp from Bua's meagre belongings.

Kalyani and Shakuntala stood apart. Shakuntala's face was a mask of consternation and anguish; without the money for cremation, Madhumati would have Bua's body placed in a sack and thrown into the river. Reading her thoughts, and fearing the same, Kalyani quietly opened a knot in her sari. She removed the few coins secreted there, and handed them to Shakuntala, saying: "*Didi*, I was saving these for my cremation."

"Oh! What a goddess!" Madhumati simpered with one of those flattering smiles she could conjure up at will. Absolved of all responsibility for the cremation, she stood up ponderously. Her aged bones creaked from sitting so long in an upright chair, and, calling upon two widows to assist her, she hobbled off to conduct business from her bed.

⚕

CHUYIA PUSHED A SIX-INCH toy boat, with a leaf stuck in it for a sail, along the river with a stick. The day that had started off for her as white, a milky, disorienting white, with its white temples and white goats and white steps, was now beating down on her in a blinding glare that skewered her to the darkest reality. Bua was dead. A frail, old woman who had once been a little girl like her. She felt she was surrounded by the dead, hounded by death, by the constant stench of funeral pyres.

With the natural acceptance of a child, Chuyia had initially taken the *ghats* and the funeral pyres in stride, viewing them as a component of city life. Rawalpur was the first big city she had seen, and to her mind all big cities were on the banks of rivers, lined with *ghats* and glowing with funeral fires. Now she wanted no part of this city of death. The monsoon-wash from the mountains muddied the blue waters with its rich silt and turned the Ganga into a raging torrent. Across the boiling river, on the other side, stretched garlands of trees, and behind them lush forests festooned with creepers that she knew were alive with birdsong and the fresh fragrance of fruit and flowers—and beyond that her village. The homesickness that had become a buried component of her being now came to the surface. How she ached for the soft comfort of her mother's flesh, for *baba*, her brothers.

Chuyia noticed a broken chain of marigold flowers between two rocks. As she picked it up, she recalled a prayer her mother had taught her to say for Prasad and Mohan by the village pond. Chuyia stepped up to the rough waves at the water's edge and, releasing the flowers into it one by one, prayed:

Oh, sacred pond; oh, holy flower!
I worship you beneath the sky.
A girl's purity is my dower;
My brothers live and blest am I.

As the flowers bobbed away, she wondered: was her life with them, as Sadananda had tried to patiently explain, just *maya*, an illusion that went *phut!* and opened into another illusion in which she was a widow? If there were better illusions in store for her, she didn't want them. She wanted to be back in her village home, back in a *maya* teeming with loved ones, with gooseberry bushes and wild leechee—orchards that miraculously produced tart, unripe mangoes and ripe mangoes more delicious than the sweet *laddoo* Bua had choked on.

Chuyia's body turned cold at the thought. She saw Bua, straight-backed, bring the yellow orb's fragrance daintily to her nose, and then shove the whole *laddoo* into her mouth. She saw the hand clapped to her mouth. And then she saw her long, serpentine neck, so thin it was almost transparent, as the squished *laddoo* slithered down her throat. The muscles of her neck distended and contracted, bulged and contracted—and then Madhumati's insistent summons called her away.

Chuyia flung herself down on the stone, racked by sobs. She had killed Bua by giving her the *laddoo*. She had murdered the sweet old woman who loved her and treated her as her best friend. When her crying was spent, she was surprised to see the toy boat with its leafy sail, still there, snagged between some pebbles and held to shore by the ripples. She picked up her stick and began pushing the boat downstream.

Shakuntala had been searching frantically for Chuyia, calling for her everywhere. She spotted her playing with her stick along the river and was at once swamped by the conflicting emotions of relief and anger.

Part of her wanted to smack the girl silly, and another to clasp her to her heart and never let her out of her sight.

Drawing near to the girl, her consternation plain in her face, she scolded, "Where did you run off to? Don't you ever listen? I've told you…"

Chuyia interrupted the flow of her scolding words and disarmed Shakuntala with the simple truth of her statement, "You're always angry."

Shakuntala lowered her gaze and collapsed to sit on the steps, feeling guilty for all the times she had been impatient with Chuyia. She felt old and drained from loss. Cut off for so long from her family, Shakuntala had made Bua her family. She sat down on the *ghats* and gently pulled Chuyia down to sit beside her.

"I was going home to my village," Chuyia confessed.

"You can't go home," Shakuntala said, her heart aching for the child. She tried to search for words to console her.

"I know," Chuyia said, before Shakuntala could say anything.

The resignation and finality in her voice tore at Shakuntala's heart. She bent forward and looked closely into the wan face.

Chuyia couldn't meet her eyes. After a moment, as two tears slipped down her cheeks, she despondently said, "Bua ate a *laddoo*."

Shakuntala recalled the yellow stains at the corners of Bua's mouth. She had wondered about it at the time but had forgotten about it in the ensuing chaos of her death.

"Don't worry," she smiled. "After eating the *laddoo*, she'll go to heaven." She added wryly, "God willing, she'll be reborn as a man!"

Chuyia scooted closer to Shakuntala and, turning, leaned her head on her chest. As the tenderness from the contact spread through her body, Shakuntala marvelled at the sweetness she felt. She tried to comfort the little girl. Chuyia's sari had slipped from her shoulder, and she lay almost doubled over. Shakuntala noticed the swelling around her breasts. She wondered if they were incipient breasts, or just a fold in the flesh from the way she was hunched over. Still awkward with the mother-role she had unwittingly assigned to herself, she pushed Chuyia up and surreptitiously glanced at her chest. There was the faintest swell; only a mother's anxious eye would notice it, she thought, smiling to herself, and then the smile froze on her lips as it occurred to her: or a man's lusting eye. She quickly pulled the girl's sari over her shoulder to cover her chest. Her concern making her voice severe, she said, "You're growing up now; keep your chest covered." Chuyia did not mind the severity: she sounded exactly like her mother, and she knew her concern for her was genuine.

They sat in silence facing the river. After a while Shakuntala asked, "How old are you?"

"Eight...Nine...I don't know."

"You don't know your birthday?"

Chuyia shook her head. "No. *Amma* said I was born in the rainy season."

"Then your birthday could be today, tomorrow. I'll tell you what; you can choose your birthday, and we will remember it. Will you like that?"

Chuyia nodded uncertainly.

Chapter Thirteen

⋈

Kalyani came down the stairs discreetly. The widows were chanting a *bhajan* in the courtyard. Rocking back and forth on their haunches, raising their tired voices in song and juggling tambourines, they filled the evening with their melancholy hymns.

Kalyani crossed the courtyard behind them and slipped into Shakuntala's room.

She stopped at the threshold. Shakuntala was mending a torn sari.

"*Didi?*" she said.

Shakuntala looked up from her work, as Kalyani came into the room and sat down on the floor. She wordlessly handed her the note from Narayan. She looked nervous. Shakuntala opened the note, and held it up to the light of the lamp. Without any preamble, she read it aloud in an even, dispassionate voice. "Kalyani, I would like to meet you tonight. At Karma Ghat. At the Shiva Temple. I will wait for you. Yours, Narayan."

As she listened to Narayan's words, Kalyani's face became flushed and she glowed with the rapture the words engendered. Shakuntala glanced at her and quickly turned her eyes away, but in that fleeing instant Kalyani knew she was pleased for her.

Shakuntala folded the note into its original creases and silently handed it back to Kalyani.

Kalyani, flustered, began to explain, "I met him with Chuyia."

"I didn't ask," Shakuntala replied dryly.

"What should I do, *didi*?" Kalyani's question was more a plea for help.

"Don't ask me," Shakuntala replied, making it plain that she had only read out the letter and what Kalyani decided to do was entirely up to her. While she was happy that Kalyani had found love, she was all too aware of the dangers such a forbidden relationship could pose for her.

Kalyani lowered her head and became thoughtful, quietly weighing the cost of going to meet Narayan against that of not going and losing this improbable, and, in all likelihood, her only chance at love.

Shakuntala left Kalyani to her internal debate and wandered out into the courtyard. She needed to be by herself. She sat quietly, a little apart from the singing widows, finding a quiet space for herself in all that noise. She finally permitted her grief to take her wherever it chose. What difference did it make whether Bua was tied in an old jute-sack and dumped into a river or if she was burnt on a pyre? An old woman, who had once been young like her, was dead: and there was no one except herself, and perhaps the child, to mourn her. The poor widow had rotted in an *ashram* even though, like herself, she came from a family of landowners who had hounded her out of her house when her husband died. His brothers most likely didn't want her to have a share in the inheritance, or their wives the care and feeding of this jinxed person whose karma it was to "eat up" her husband. Bua had told her that her two young sons had immediately been sent to another village, and whatever feelings they once had for their mother had dissipated over time. Bua was not allowed to write to her grandchildren because her sons found out that she sat on the streets of the Holy City with a begging bowl. Who had turned her into a beggar if not them? Bua had been widowed when she was about thirty-five. She had sung her lungs out till she was seventy. What for? A cup of rice and an occasional cowrie-coin flung at her? An old woman, who had once been young like her. And when she herself was an old crone, a younger widow would look at her and think, *Some day, I too will be an old crone like her and I will die un-mourned.* She remembered the time-honoured words known by all Hindu women, exhorting that the sight of the widow itself was something inauspicious, so inauspicious that if sighted at the beginning of an auspicious venture, the venture itself had to be postponed. Shakuntala felt a tug-of-war within her. Her common sense pitched against these age-old traditions practised simply because it was always so—these thoughts were running in opposing directions in her mind and heart.

KALYANI LET HERSELF OUT THE DOOR of the *ashram*. It was quite late. She walked swiftly along a dark alley and stopped at a Krishna shrine at the end of a narrow gully, which ran along an open drain. The temple was fragrant with incense. There was a labyrinth of small spaces that appeared to occupy different levels, and the interior was bathed in the play of light and shadow from the flames of a hundred steadily burning oil lamps. They sat in rows on mantels, ledges, shelves, on the sides of steps and in alcoves, and the light they cast on the adobe walls was golden and calming. There was no one about at this hour, except the flute-playing Krishna ensconced in his sanctum. Kalyani prostrated herself before the image of the God who was filled with love and who loved with such abandon, marrying 8000 women who craved him for a husband and choosing from among his doting *gopis* whichever caught his fleeting fancy. She asked for the compassionate god's permission to visit her lover, and at the same time for his forgiveness for what she was about to do. She asked for his blessing.

Kalyani went to an extinguished oil lamp and with her finger lifted the soot from its wick. She carefully underlined each eye with the kohl on her fingertip: the temple was well known for the quality of its soot-kohl and sold it in tiny vials. She picked up an oil *pradip*, closed her eyes for a moment and took a deep, quavering breath. She stepped out into the dark and, with the light from the *pradip*, made her way down to the river.

The river was a dark ribbon, except for the temple fires it reflected. Wisps of white smoke curled up against the black, star-pricked sky. A boat glided silently along the river. A gentle breeze carried to her the haunting, long-drawn-out notes of a flute. She stilled to listen, certain it was the same *bansari*-player she and Gulabi had heard in the boat that other night.

Further down the river, at Karma Ghat, Narayan waited patiently for Kalyani. At fitful intervals he played the flute, or paced up and down along the river. He dared not let his hopes rise too high; he had a good idea of how much Kalyani would risk in coming to him.

A temple, small and deserted, lay in ruins low on the *ghats*, its east wall open to the river. A black stone *lingam* nestled among the gigantic roots of an ancient banyan tree. Narayan waited beneath the enormous spread of its branches.

Kalyani approached their meeting place, her head covered, her feet bare, still holding the *pradip*. She saw Narayan at once, sitting with his feet up on a stone bench and leaning against the tree; he was playing his flute. Kalyani felt her body drain of strength and her blood thud in her ear. Taken aback by the effect his physical presence had on her, Kalyani stood rooted to the earth and stared at him. When he finished playing and put his flute down, she announced her presence. "I'm here."

Narayan turned to Kalyani. She was a vision of beauty in her widow's white, lit by moonlight. He walked slowly towards her saying, "*Neepam dhrashtva harıtkapısham kesherre rardhyarudhe—ravirbhuta prathamkukulah kandalishvanukaccham.* On the banks of the river, where the *kadamba* flowers bloom...."

Kalyani, not understanding his words, looked confused.

His face radiating his joy, Narayan gazed at her and translated, "The *kadamba* is a flower so fragrant that people swoon in its presence."

Kalyani blushed. They sat down, well apart, on a stone ledge beneath the tree. It was lined with oil lamps. Kalyani looked straight ahead; she dared not look at Narayan.

"It's from Kalidas's poem, '*Meghdoot*,'" Narayan explained, turning to Kalyani and gazing at her clean profile.

Kalyani set her *pradip* down between them, and, keeping her head lowered and glancing shyly at Narayan from under her lids, confessed, "I can't read. Shakuntala-*didi* read your letter."

Narayan was utterly enchanted. Every new facet of her was a revelation. Had she rattled off an obscure Sanskrit poem in riposte to his, he would have been equally enchanted.

"Do you know what "*Meghdoot* is?" he asked.

Kalyani shook her head, "No."

Narayan stood up and in an expansive, extravagant gesture stretched out his hand to the sky. "In Sanskrit, '*megh*' means a rain cloud and '*doot*,' a messenger. The poem is about the pain of separation between lovers."

As Kalyani raised her head to look at the clouds that were scuttling past the moon, the sari slid off her hair and her lovely features were lit by the candles and edged by moonlight. Narayan was mesmerized by her beauty and fell silent.

"Go on," urged Kalyani.

Silently communicating his intent, Narayan glanced at her and stood up. Kalyani also rose, and as they walked together he continued the story.

"The lover tells the cloud it resembles Lord Vishnu,

disguised as Lord Krishna: 'Gleaming with peacock feathers.'"

"And the cloud hears him? How is that possible?" Kalyani, emboldened by his chatter, teased.

"If we believe that a statue of a god can hear us, why not a cloud?"

This Kalyani understood. Now she had a question of her own for Narayan. "Are you gentry? A *seth*?" she asked hesitantly.

"Would it matter if I was?" said Narayan

"Yes," she said so softly, Narayan wondered if she'd answered at all.

To tide over the sudden unease Narayan felt, he volunteered information about himself. "I just finished my law exams. I was studying in Calcutta." And this time when he glanced at her, he took in the worn condition of her patched sari.

"When did you become a widow?" he asked gently, his voice hesitant.

They had wandered down to the river's edge. Kalyani picked up a stone and threw it into the water; she intently watched the spreading ripples. "I don't remember. Maybe when I was nine," she said, uncomfortable with her status as a widow.

"Was your husband good to you?" asked Narayan

"I never met him," Kalyani answered matter-of-factly.

Narayan became quiet. They sat down side by side, the river lapping at the step below them.

"Is there anyone else? Uh—in your house?" Kalyani asked awkwardly.

"My mother, my father and Sadhuram, our old servant...my three younger sisters are in a boarding school in Nainital," answered Narayan. He guessed what Kalyani was driving at, and put her at her ease. "No, I'm not married," he said, laughing.

Kalyani blushed, and her lips twitched in a smile. She was immensely relieved to learn this, but her relief was quickly replaced by surprise that such a desirable man was still unattached. "Good God! Why ever not?" she exclaimed.

Shrugging, Narayan answered, "My father says, 'Childhood is a time for play, not for marriage.'"

"You're a child?" Kalyani teased. "And your mother?"

"If she had her way, I'd have a daughter as old as Chuyia."

"Your mother's right. That's how things are," said Kalyani reasonably.

"That's how things were. Many of the old traditions are dying out," Narayan said, speaking with a sobriety that underlined his assurance.

Kalyani looked shocked. "All of them?" Before Narayan could answer, she added with conviction, "But what is good should not be allowed to die."

Narayan looked at her in amazement, surprised that a person who had suffered so much because of these very traditions would defend them in any way. "And who will decide what is good and what is not?" he asked her.

"You!" Kalyani exclaimed playfully.

They smiled at each other, and their eyes met, lingering shyly and tenderly. They sat in companionable silence, and watched the pink of dawn light spill into the river.

THE WIDOWS LINED THE RIVER AT Tulsi Ghat, their teeth chattering in the cold. It was early dawn. A line of the palest pink edged the horizon. Using pulleys rigged to wicker baskets, in each of which burned a lamp, the widows raised the baskets. They prayed to the yellowing moon overhead, as trays heaped with marigolds and candles in their centres floated by. Chuyia wandered among the widows. A lumpy shape, covered in a white sheet strewn with flowers, followed the trays. Chuyia wondered if it was a corpse. She thought of Bua. The widows saw so little change in their routines, she would have enjoyed pulling up the baskets.

Later that afternoon, the sky crackled with thunder and rain fell in torrential sheets. Chuyia came down the stairs from Kalyani's room and ran quickly across the courtyard, trying not to get wet. By the time she entered Shakuntala's room, she was soaked. Shakuntala looked up wearily; she was cutting dried coconut leaves.

"*Didi*, when do we get food? I'm hungry," said Chuyia.

"Today we fast. It is Maha Shivratri. No food, no water. Come sit here," said Shakuntala, bracing herself, expecting Chuyia to protest.

When the protest didn't materialize, Shakuntala asked, "What's wrong? No tantrums?"

Chuyia merely shrugged. She sat down beside Shakuntala and began to toy idly with a coconut leaf.

This dulling of Chuyia's feisty spirit concerned Shakuntala. "You're getting used to this life," she observed quietly.

Chuyia was restive. "I have to go," she said. "Kalyani's telling me about Kalidas."

Shakuntala was surprised by this information and stared open-mouthed at Chuyia. "What?"

"A poet," Chuyia explained.

Shakuntala's stern features softened, and for the first time since Bua's death she smiled. Chuyia ran out the door, eager to get back to Kalyani and her stories. Shakuntala wished she had stayed a bit.

CHUYIA AND KALYANI LAY ON their mats in the covered portion of the balcony, looking contentedly at the rain. Its intensity had lessened, and the deafening clatter they had been subjected to when it pelted down on the corrugated-iron roof was reduced to a soothing drumming. Kalyani pointed to a cloud and instructed Chuyia, "'*Megh*' means cloud, and '*doot*' a messenger."

"The Cloud Messenger," repeated Chuyia.

"Come on, let's send a message," suggested Kalyani. She closed her eyes in concentration, expecting Chuyia to do the same. When she opened them, Chuyia was stretched out on her stomach, her head resting on her hands, looking glum.

"Did you send your message?" Kalyani asked.

"I don't want to send one."

Kalyani's heart ached for Chuyia. The girl had abandoned all hope of returning to her family and her carefree life in the village. Kalyani remembered the slow draining of hope within her those many years ago when she began to realize that she could never go back.

Madhumati's imperious voice called out, "Kalyani!"

They exchanged a glance, but neither stirred.

"Why don't you send one?" urged Kalyani, wanting Chuyia to reconsider.

Kunti took over from Madhumati. "Kalyani! Have you gone deaf?" she yelled irritably from the courtyard, getting drenched in the rain. "*Didi* wants you."

Kalyani sighed. She got up slowly and went down the stairs, where she was met by a cold, wet and scolding Kunti.

Kalyani stood in the door of Madhumati's room, watching her feed chickpeas, one at a time, to her scraggly looking parrot. She didn't bother to look at her.

Madhumati crooned, "You are lucky, Mitthu. You don't have to fast." She laughed at her own joke and fed him another chickpea.

"Yes, *didi*," Kalyani announced her presence.

"Come on in, child," Madhumati said sweetly. She waddled to her bed and pulled a new white sari out from under her pillow. She held it out to Kalyani. "Here, this is for you," she said, as if she were bequeathing a family heirloom.

Kalyani, knowing full well the significance of this "gift," did not care to conceal her resentment. She took the sari indifferently and turned to go.

"Wait, child," Madhumati said, stopping her. "Come, sit next to me," she coaxed. Kalyani looked at her with foreboding. The last time Madhumati had given her a new sari and spoken to her in these syrupy tones, she had been sent to a house outside Rawalpur, where she had been brutalized and Gulabi had had to come to her rescue. It had taken her a long time to recover from the gang rape, and a penitent Madhumati had become more selective of her clients.

Kalyani had somehow learned to compartmentalize her life. Her childhood was in one box, and occasionally she opened it and let the happy memories spill out. Her meetings with Narayan were locked up in another box she kept close to her heart and opened frequently. She kept her nocturnal calls in a recessed box hidden even from herself and allowed it open only when she was doing business for Madhumati.

"Learn to live like a lotus," Krishna had said in the *Gita*, "untouched by the filthy water." Kalyani had taken these words to heart and had learned to live by them. This way, her life was made bearable, and the transactions with the clients did not poison her day-to-day hours or her relationships with others.

"You must take care of yourself," Madhumati cooed, and Kalyani noticed she was stroking her thigh. "You are the jewel of this house," the woman said, gazing at her fondly. "If you are happy, our clients are happy. And when they're happy, I am happy!"

Kalyani couldn't take it anymore. "This is an *ashram*, *didi*, not a brothel," she said quietly.

The affection and good cheer drained from Madhumati's flabby face, as spite and cunning narrowed her eyes. Kalyani slipped away before Madhumati could get back at her.

Chapter Fourteen

Chuyia became their secret emissary, ferrying little notes from Narayan and conveying Kalyani's verbal answers to him. She took her role seriously and delighted in it, and that is how, some days later, Kalyani came to be riding in an elegant four-wheeled carriage with Narayan at dusk. Narayan directed the driver to take a turn, and they clip-clopped along a stately boulevard in the British cantonment. Graceful eucalyptus trees stood erect in orderly rows in their appointed grooves along the pavement, and the bases of their trunks were painted white. A ribbon of red paint circled the white at the top, and the same red ran along the side of the pavement. The atmosphere was serene and orderly: a world apart from the crowded, raucous city with its temples, food stalls, animal and human traffic, lean-tos and open drains.

Kalyani sat at a suitable distance from Narayan, which, given the narrow width of the carriage, was not large. She was overwhelmed by the novelty of the experience. She touched the rich leather of the seat in wonder, then turned and lifted the closed blind to peer timidly out the carriage window as they passed ornate stucco mansions, lined with formal rows of box shrubs, sitting amidst immaculately kept grounds. Her head was uncovered, her dark hair shining, and her young face fresh and dewy.

Narayan, beside himself with joy to have Kalyani in the carriage with him, watched her reactions eagerly. "We are at the edge of the city," he explained. "Where the British live."

Kalyani looked at him apprehensively, worried that she did not belong here; what if someone recognized that she was a widow?

Narayan guessed the cause of her alarm. "They don't care if you're a widow," he assured her.

"Why? Don't they have widows?" Kalyani asked.

"Of course they do. But not like ours; they don't treat them like we do," said Narayan. "It must be hard for you," he said, unable to conceal the compassion that laced his voice.

Kalyani kept her head slightly bowed and did not look at Narayan. "Sometimes yes, sometimes no," she said. "'Learn to live like a lotus…Untouched by the filthy water it grows in.' Krishna*ji* says it in the *Gita*."

Narayan stared at Kalyani thoughtfully. "Krishna was a god. Not everyone can live like the lotus flower," he said.

"Yes they can," Kalyani stated simply. She avoided meeting his eyes and looked out the window instead.

They rode in silence. After a while, Kalyani shyly turned towards Narayan and, their bodies swaying with the movement of the carriage, lightly touched a black stain on his shirt pocket: "What's that?"

Narayan was sheepish. "It's ink. I didn't have time to change. I was applying for a job in Calcutta."

Kalyani was stunned by the revelation; it had never occurred to her that Narayan could be anywhere else. She stared fixedly at her lap.

"What's wrong?" Narayan asks.

"When do you go?" Her voice was small.

"As soon as they call me."

Kalyani distractedly wound the edge of her sari in and out of her fingers. "And when will you be back?" She gave him a sidelong glance.

Narayan reached over and gently untangled the fabric she had wound around her hand, and took both her hands in his.

"I'm not going anywhere without you," he said with quiet certainty, as if he were uttering an oath.

Kalyani looked into his eyes, and then lowered her regard. Narayan edged a little closer and gripped her hands more tightly. Kalyani felt her blood turn to water and her legs tremble: then everything in the world ceased to exist except his hand in hers.

Late that night, Kalyani quietly entered Shakuntala's room. The floor was covered with the old widows Shakuntala had taken under her wing, now that Bua was no longer there to take care of. Kalyani crept over to Chuyia's mat and lightly touched the girl's heel. Chuyia's foot jerked reflexively, but she stayed asleep. Kalyani knelt beside her and shook her gently by the shoulder to waken her. When this, too, failed to rouse her, Kalyani leaned in close to Chuyia's face and blew on her. Chuyia awoke, and a huge smile broke on her sleepy face as she saw Kalyani hovering over her.

Chuyia quietly followed Kalyani up the stairs to her

room. Kaalu greeted them excitedly. They lay down on their mats with Kaalu prancing between their legs, licking their laughing faces. Kalyani, propped up on an elbow, stroked the spiky stubble on Chuyia's head and whispered to her the wonderful things she had seen, what she and Narayan had said to each other, and all the other details of her magical evening with the man she loved best in the whole world.

"More than Krishna?" Chuyia asked.

Kalyani became thoughtful. "Yes. More than Krishna," she said after a pause, and became confused. "Krishna is a god. I can't love him in the same way," she said.

Chuyia looked at Kalyani, wide-eyed, and through a kind of osmosis felt what she felt: a strange, heavy sweetness filled her body, and she became still, intent, as if listening to music.

Chuyia felt closer to Kalyani than ever before and she wanted to know everything about her. Gently, her mood contemplative with the music within her, Chuyia began to ask Kalyani about her past. It comforted her to discover that Kalyani's story was much like her own. Kalyani's family was very poor and had no landholdings. She had two brothers and two sisters, all older than she. Her mother had always been weak, and the five pregnancies had taken their toll on her health. Kalyani's mother had died before she had reached her first birthday.

With three daughters on his hands, her father had been anxious to marry them off. Word of Kalyani's beauty had spread, and she was married off to the highest bidder, a man of sixty, when she was six. After that, her life story was much like Chuyia's. She had lived in the village with her family. Her husband had become ill, and Kalyani had accompanied him to the *ghats*. He had died a few days after they had come to Rawalpur and the widowed child had been dumped at the *ashram*. Kalyani said she had also fought and screamed like Chuyia at first, but had soon realized that it wouldn't do her any good.

"They didn't shave your head?" Chuyia asked.

"They did, but Madhu-*didi* let me grow it back."

"Why?" Chuyia asked, running her fingers through Kalyani's silky strands.

"You're as inquisitive as your namesake, aren't you?" Kalyani, who spoke to Chuyia as an equal, seldom adopted the adult, dismissive tone of voice she used now. "You will understand when you're older."

The mechanizations of the adult world were a mystery to Chuyia. She had been told this so often that she didn't question the statement. Experience had taught her that no amount of pleading would persuade adults to divulge their secrets. "Madhu-*didi* is kind to you. She likes you," Chuyia said

Kalyani kept quiet. Madhumati had been only too delighted to take in such a young beauty and had immediately made arrangements to sell her services. She fetched an unheard-of price, for in addition to her rare beauty, she had been a virgin-widow. Kalyani had been nine at the time.

"Will Madhu-*didi* let me grow my hair if I ask her?"

Kalyani raised herself on an elbow and looked earnestly at Chuyia. "Promise me you will never ask her that."

Chuyia looked at her in surprise. "Why?"

"You trust me, don't you?"

Overwhelmed and upset by Kalyani's uncharacteristic *gravitas*, Chuyia nodded.

"Then say it. Say, 'I promise I will never ask Madhu-*didi* to let my hair grow.'"

Chuyia, perplexed, solemnly repeated the words. "I promise I will never ask Madhu-*didi* to let my hair grow."

"You won't break your promise?"

"No."

Kalyani kissed her forehead and lay back, relaxed.

After that, Kalyani and Chuyia talked far into the night, giggling and sharing stories, and then, as is the way with children, Chuyia suddenly fell asleep. Kalyani lay awake, lost in romantic fantasies.

᷾

SUNSHINE FLOODED THE ROOM. Although Narayan had slept very little, he got up refreshed and full of vigour. He put his favourite morning *raag* on the gramophone and hummed along with Omkarnath Thakur, shaking his head at the maestro's virtuosity, as he worked his shaving cream into lather. He was applying shaving cream to his face when there was a sharp knock on his door. "Come in, Ma," he said, recognizing the knock.

Wrapped up in a bright yellow sari and covered in gold jewelry, Bhagwati sailed into the room. "I was waiting for you to get up," she said, picking up Narayan's clothes from the various places they were strewn and moving about restlessly. She looked disturbed.

Narayan smiled at her, amused, as he wiped the lather off his face with a towel.

"Did you have a fight with *baba*?"

"He's never here to have a fight with!" Bhagwati complained. She sighed and continued to walk about the room, folding and refolding his clothes, attacking the few specks of dust Sadhuram had spared. She noticed Gandhi's photograph was hung a bit off-centre and she straightened it. She stared at the Mahatma.

"What does he preach?" she asked, curious.

"That's Gandhi*ji*. Not some crooked priest, Ma," Narayan corrected her.

"So what does he say, then?"

"He talks about freedom, about truth."

"To talk about freedom is easy, but to live by it, is not," Bhagwati replied tartly. There was silence between them for a moment.

Bhagwati sat down on the chair at his desk and, looking at him directly, divulged the reason for her visit. She had rehearsed her choice of words. "The girl's father is getting impatient."

"What?" said Narayan, as if he had no idea what she was talking about.

"Turn off that gramophone!" said Bhagwati, exasperated by his attitude.

Narayan complied.

"I want a straightforward yes or no. They won't wait forever."

"No!" Narayan said definitively.

Bhagwati's face fell. She looked perplexed. She could not understand why her son, amenable in all other respects, refused to comply with his parents' wish to see him settled. By now he should have provided them grandsons! He had received fine offers. She had shown him the photographs of only the prettier girls, the ones with substantial dowries. He had rejected them offhand.

"Don't you want to set up a family?"

"It's not like setting yogurt," Narayan quipped. Then he flopped down on his bed and, reclining comfortably against the pillows, pulled out his flute. He began to play a cheerful folk song.

Bhagwati, riled, grabbed the flute out of his hands.

"If this is your attitude, how will I ever find a girl for you?" She was almost in tears.

"You don't have to. I've found her myself," Narayan said calmly.

Bhagwati's face registered shock. "Really?" she said in disbelief.

Narayan nodded "yes." Bhagwati's irate features underwent a transformation as she relaxed. She touched his face tenderly and, leaning in, weighed in with the questions.

"Who is she? Do I know her?"

"No."

"Is she Brahmin?"

"She could be."

Bhagwati looked at him sharply, "You want to marry her and you don't even know her caste?"

"Ma, caste doesn't matter to me. You should know that by now."

It was the influence of this wretched Gandhi. "Well, tell me more. Is she fair?"

Narayan laughed. "Is that all that matters? Light skin?"

"Other things also matter," Bhagwati said, offended.

"Like what?"

"Morals, health, family. Well, is she?"

Narayan smiled. "Yes, she's fair."

He became serious. "Ma, she's beautiful." His words ended in an involuntary sigh.

Bhagwati's expression softened, as she gazed upon her son. If he loved the girl so much, she would love her too.

"Even if she was dark, she'd be beautiful," Narayan said poetically.

"You aren't lying, are you?" Bhagwati asked suspiciously.

"No, Ma. She's as fair as you'd wish."

Bhagwati was relieved. Her son had an eye for pretty girls; she should have known he wouldn't land her with some swarthy creature she'd be ashamed of toting around. Aloud she said, "Your father will not like this insult."

"What insult?"

"It's a smack to our faces. We have done every-thing for you, yet you don't trust us to make the right choice for you?!"

"It's not a question of trust, Ma. It's just that... I've found her."

Bhagwati sat on the bed near his feet. She understood what was left unsaid. She began stroking his legs in a light massage as she was used to. "Who is she?"

"She's a widow," said Narayan.

Bhagwati's head jerked up. She stared at him in hor-ror, and then she covered her face with her hands. It couldn't be true. "You are joking," she said and smacked Narayan's feet in disgust.

Narayan looked at her calmly.

"*Hai* Bhagwan! You're serious! How will we show our face to the world?" Weeping and wiping her tears on her sari, she scolded him, "Gandhi has turned you into a lunatic! Marry a widow? How can you even think of it? It's a sin! You should know that!"

Narayan had expected this reaction. He understood exactly how intolerable the thought of his marrying a widow was to her, and she could be relied upon to enact tempestuous scenes. In the end, though, she could deny him nothing. He was her only son, and she adored him. He said, "It is not as terrible as you think, Ma—old ways and ideas have changed. Raja Ramohan Roy says widows should get remarried."

Bhagwati wiped her nose on her sari and retorted disgustedly, "And Raja Whoever—what does he know about our traditions? What will your father say?"

"He'll be pleased. He's a freethinker," Narayan replied calmly.

"You'll find out how freethinking he is when he hears this! He'll throw you out of the house! *Hai* Bhagwan, show mercy," Bhagwati said, weeping. Narayan offered her his handkerchief, but she pushed it away, wailing, "Stop it!"

Narayan picked up his flute again and began to play.

Bhagwati snatched the flute from his hand. "Oh, God! What will happen to your sisters? Have you thought of that? Who will marry them?! No one wants a girl whose family spits on tradition and religion!"

"They're pretty, they'll bring big dowries. I wouldn't worry about them."

Bhagwati was outraged. "You wouldn't worry? As long as you get what you want, your sisters can rot in hell?" She smacked her head and thumped her chest. "Oh Lord, break the ground and swallow me! You might as well give me poison!"

"You should get a gold medal for drama, Ma," Narayan teased, trying to jolly her out of her state.

"You think this is drama? I will swallow my diamonds and bleed to death! I will stab myself with a knife," she wailed, jabbing herself with the flute.

Narayan got up quickly and wrestled the flute from her, saying, "Stop it, Ma. You'll hurt yourself." He tried to embrace her.

She pushed him away. "You'll know what drama is when I kill myself!" she shrieked, and ran from the room, weeping.

Narayan placed his hands behind his head and, reclining on the pillows, closed his eyes. "She is beautiful," he said softly, to the empty room.

Chapter Fifteen

❋

Gulabi, in a breathtaking clash of colours, stood at the window eating a dish of *puris* and potatoes from a bowl made out of dried palm leaves.

"You look like my Mitthu today," Madhumati mumbled from her bed.

Gulabi cast a preening glance at her vivid-green sari and peach blouse with its yellow trim. She ran a swarthy hand over the ornaments in her hair, fastidiously adjusting them.

"But my Mitthu is better-looking," Madhumati mumbled conclusively.

Madhumati had adopted her usual position for this time of day. Stretched out on her stomach like a satiated sea-lion, her head turned to one side, she lay still, listening to Gulabi's gossip and offering an occasional comment. Chuyia was at her regular task, dutifully massaging Madhumati by walking up and down her buttocks and thighs. Every short while, her nose picked up the spicy fragrances wafting in from the window, and her attention wandered to the food being daintily picked at by Gulabi with her fingers.

Poking her arms through the bars, Gulabi offered the dish to Madhumati. "Have some, *didi*?" she said, between mouthfuls.

"I've been farting non-stop since morning," Madhumati complained, refusing the offer. "Perhaps I ate too much last night." Lifting her behind slightly, she passed a bubbling volley of wind.

Awestruck, Chuyia wondered how she did it—she could summon up the artillery at will.

Chuyia carefully negotiated Madhumati's buttocks and came to stand on her back. She stared as Gulabi licked the juice from the vegetables off her fingers and all the way up her forearm. Gulabi caught her watching and offered her half-eaten *puri* to Chuyia.

"Here, eat some," she said.

Hanging onto the bar above her with one hand, Chuyia reached for it, but was stopped by Madhumati's shrill cry. "Are you mad?" she scolded Gulabi. "Giving a widow forbidden food!"

Gulabi merely shrugged her peachy shoulders and finished off the food.

"So what? I'll eat a hundred *puris* at Kalyani's wedding," Chuyia defiantly boasted.

Gulabi's mouth dropped open in disbelief, while Madhumati's back gave a convulsive little jerk beneath Chuyia's feet.

Chuyia, unaware of the significance of what she had let slip, continued treading on Madhumati's back.

"Whose wedding?" asked Madhumati in a childishly sweet voice that matched Chuyia's.

"Kalyani's wedding," Chuyia replied innocently.

"And when is her wedding?" asked Madhumati, a dangerous edge creeping into her sweetness.

"Don't know," Chuyia replied simply, shrugging her shoulders.

Madhumati and Gulabi exchanged a look.

Madhumati snorted, "She'll get married over my dead body! Widows don't get married."

"But she will. I know she will," Chuyia insisted.

"No! She won't! Now get off," ordered Madhumati.

Chuyia grew rigid with anger, and her face flushed a dusky red. Who was Madhumati to deny her friend her marriage, her chance at happiness? Chuyia had invested a lot of hope in Kalyani's newfound circumstances. Embroiled in Kalyani's dreams, she had allowed herself to dream again. If Kalyani could escape her circumstances and remarry, then Chuyia might some day manage to do so also and break away from the *ashram*. Now she saw their combined hopes dashed by Madhumati's ugly denial. She began stomping on Madhumati's back, harder and faster and shouting, "She will! She will! SHE WILL! Go drown yourself! Liar!"

Gulabi stared through the bars, astonished.

Madhumati raised her head and bellowed, "Kalyani! Come at once!"

Hearing Kalyani so harshly summoned, and realizing what might lie in store for her, Chuyia lost control and in hysterical frenzy began jumping up and down as hard as she could on Madhumati's hapless body, screaming at the top of her lungs, over and over, "Madhu Fatty! Liar Fatty! Bitchy Fatty!"

Traumatized by shock, and in pain from the pounding she was being subjected to by Chuyia's stomping feet, Madhumati screamed in alarm. She waved her massive arms behind her back like unwieldy fly swatters, trying to dislodge Chuyia. Gulabi, unable to reach Chuyia through the bars of the window, added her own ineffective screeches to those of Madhumati, "Get off the old bitch! She'll die!"

"Get this devil off me!" Madhumati howled.

Kunti came running in to see what was causing all the commotion. She froze, horrified, as she took in the scene.

"Don't just stand there, bitch, do something!" bawled Madhumati, and galvanized by Madhumati's agonized holler, Kunti scooted off to fetch Shakuntala. Kunti knew she was the only one to control Chuyia.

Madhumati, trapped beneath Chuyia's punishing feet as she hopped all over her stranded girth, groaned and tried in vain to grab hold of Chuyia's ankles. Reaching through the bars and bellowing, Gulabi ineffectually flayed her stubby, muscular arms.

Shakuntala came running in and, wresting Chuyia's grasp loose from the balance bar above the bed, pulled Chuyia off of Madhumati. She carried her, purple-faced and screaming, into the courtyard, which was by now filled with excitedly chattering widows. Chuyia wrapped her arms around Shakuntala's neck, but the strength of her cursing and the gush of tears coursing down her wet cheeks did not diminish.

Shakuntala carried the hysterical girl over to the well, set her down and dumped a full bucket of cold water over

Chuyia's head, saying, "Chuyia, that's enough...Chuyia, stop..."

The cold shower had no effect on Chuyia and Shakuntala doused her with another bucketful of water. Chuyia kept screaming hysterically, "Madhu Fatty! Liar Fatty! Bitchy Fatty!" and pumped her fists in vehement accompaniment to her curses.

Shakuntala grabbed Chuyia by the sides of her face and shouted, "Chuyia, ENOUGH!"

Chuyia's eyes were wild, but she quieted and stood there, panting painfully, and looking like a drowned rat as she gazed beseechingly at Shakuntala. They were both distracted just then by the spectacle of Madhumati laboriously climbing the steps to Kalyani's terrace. The other widows also turned to stare, as Madhumati determinedly negotiated the steps one at a time, a woman on a mission.

Madhumati reached the terrace, sweating and breathing hard. She stepped through the door of the staircase and called for Kalyani.

Kalyani, trembling in fear, came to her door and faced Madhumati. Her dark hair hung in wet strands down her back.

Madhumati spoke to her in low, angry tones. "Chuyia says you're getting married?"

Kalyani nodded her affirmation.

"Have you gone mad? Nobody will marry a widow."

Kalyani spoke with calm certainty. "He will."

Madhumati gave a loud snort of disdain. "Shameless! You'll sink yourself and us! We'll be cursed. We must live in purity, to die in purity," said Madhumati, disregarding the hypocrisy in preaching this to a young woman forced into prostitution against her will.

Kalyani had lived too long and painfully with this double standard and was ready to confront Madhumati.

"Then why did you send me across the river?" she asked quietly.

Madhumati was outraged that Kalyani would call her actions into question.

"For survival! And how we survive here, no one can question. Not even God!" she raged.

Before Kalyani knew what was happening, Madhumati grabbed her by her hair, and dragged her to the *barsati*, the storeroom next to Kalyani's room. Withdrawing from her sari a pair of scissors, she sawed off a hank of hair in a surprisingly swift movement. Kalyani sank to her knees in shock, too numb to resist. Madhumati proceeded to hack off the rest of her hair until Kalyani was left with only sparse tufts. Kalyani sat immobilized, like a fledgling bird fallen from its nest.

Her destructive mission completed, Madhumati shut the door on the cowering girl and turned the key in the huge padlock. She tied the key to her sari and turned her attention to the upturned faces of the widows gathered in the courtyard below.

Madhumati stood at the balustrade looking crazed, the whites of her bloodshot eyes abnormally large. "We would have burned in hell because of her. I've saved you all!" she justified her brutality. "Let's see the whore get married now!"

The widows gaped at her, speechless. Shakuntala turned to Chuyia. "Is this true?" she asked

"Yes," Chuyia confirmed with some heat. "Kalyani is getting married!"

Shakuntala shushed her, "Keep your voice down," and the two of them walked dispiritedly to Shakuntala's room, leaving the other widows to gawk at Madhumati's huge frame, lumbering down the steps.

Chuyia tugged at Shakuntala's sari. "*Didi*? You'll let Kalyani out, won't you?" she pleaded.

"To even think of remarriage is a sin," Shakuntala replied, her thoughts in turmoil—her love for Kalyani at odds with her deeply held religious beliefs.

"Why?" Chuyia asked innocently.

"Ask God," Shakuntala snapped, impatient with herself for doubting what she believed was written in the scriptures.

Chuyia, deeply hurt, ran off without a word.

Shakuntala's shoulders drooped with weariness. She could not summon the energy to call her back, explain that she was not angry at her.

After a while, she sat at her table, leafing through the religious texts, trying to find passages that mentioned the decrees governing the conduct and status of widows. According to the Manusmriti, the foremost Sanskrit text in the orthodox tradition, a widow's head is shaved, her ornaments removed, and she is expected to remain in perpetual mourning. She is to observe fasts, give up eating "hot" foods in order to cool her sexual energy, avoid auspicious occasions because she is considered inauspicious (for having caused her husband's death), and to remain celibate, devout and loyal to her husband's memory.

The later Vriddha Hirata was more explicit. She should give up chewing betel nut, wearing perfumes, flowers, ornaments and dyed clothes, taking food from a vessel of bronze, taking two meals a day, applying collyrium to the eyes; she should wear only a white garment, curb her senses and anger, and sleep on the ground.

Her thoughts in turmoil, Shakuntala stood staring out her window. The scandalized widows had again grouped around Madhumati. She sat on her *takth*, her scalp sweating, red-faced from the exertion of climbing up and down the stairs to the *barsati*. Kunti was bent over her, solicitously wiping the perspiration from her neck and exposed shoulder, and Snehlata was hunkered down on the *takth*, slowly wielding the palm leaf fan. The monsoon's strength was waning, but it was still very humid.

What she had read only affirmed what she knew and accepted—nowhere did she find anything that might redeem Kalyani; remarriage would condemn her husband's soul to hell and curse the karmas of all his family. Despite her unquestioning acceptance of the *Dharma Shastras*, that widowhood is the punishment for a sinful existence in the past, Kalyani's plight shook her belief in the laws.

She closed the curtain and withdrew from the window. She spread her mat against the wall and lay down; it was something she never did at this time of day. Memories of her life before she became a widow, which she had suppressed over the years as a part of her life that was done with and because it was a sin to remember, edged into her consciousness. She let them flood in.

Shakuntala's birth had been something of a surprise to her parents in their late middle-years. They already had four strapping sons, and the daughter was welcomed as Goddess Lakshmi, harbinger of prosperity and happiness. Her family owned a fair amount of land, and her father was a respected figure in their village. Her brothers doted upon her. They involved her in all kinds of activities girls in her village generally weren't allowed to do. They taught her how to read, and she could recite multiplications up to twenty. She had a sharp mind, and soon she was reading the books they brought home.

Her parents were determined to make a good match for her in a family that would treat her kindly and permit her the activities she was used to. Shakuntala stayed rather longer with her parents than most families would have thought prudent. Just as her parents were beginning to worry that they wouldn't find a suitable husband before she reached puberty, they learned of a young widower in a nearby village who was ready to take a new wife. Like all young girls in the village, Shakuntala looked forward to marriage, and by fourteen her head was spinning with romantic fantasies.

Their horoscopes matched, and the marriage was quickly agreed upon. As was customary, the bride's family took care of all expenses. Her father presented the groom with a handsome dowry that exceeded his family's expectations.

Shakuntala closed her eyes and, like Bua, visualized her wedding feast: huge platters filled with fried, puffed up *puris*, spicy vegetables, fragrant mounds of saffron rice and all kinds of pickles, fruit juices and fresh palm toddy.

Trays of almond and cashew fudge cut up in diamond shapes and steel *thalis* heaped with glossy *laddoos*, the top of the mounds covered with silver leaf that evaporated on the tongue. Like Bua, she could taste the *laddoos* and her mouth filled with saliva. She smiled, sending up a little prayer of thanks that Bua had finally eaten her *laddoo* before dying.

What a paltry thing to deny an old woman, Shakuntala thought, and then her mind settled on a clutch of paltry things that were denied to widows in order to preserve their purity.

God preserve her from their wretched perception of purity, she thought. But for her brothers' charity, she would have been prostituted like Kalyani was.

Shakuntala's thoughts returned to the past. Her husband was young, only thirteen years older than she. Though he had grieved deeply for his first wife, when a year had passed, he found that his heart had not been hardened by his loss, and he was ready to open himself to Shakuntala.

The first year they were together, her husband took things slowly with her, and she blossomed from a girl into a beautiful young woman. Over the course of the next few years, they fell deeply in love. Her mother-in-law, hopeful that Shakuntala would be the instrument by which her son would fulfill his debt to their forefathers by reproducing sons, treated her graciously and lovingly. However, as the years passed, Shakuntala's mother-in-law began to blame Shakuntala for her failure to produce any children. She became increasingly hateful toward her barren daughter-in-law. Though the love between

Shakuntala and her husband was full of passion, each month Shakuntala was disappointed to see the depressing evidence of her failed fertility. She desperately longed for a child.

Shakuntala had just turned thirty when her husband began to spit blood. He wasted before her eyes. Toward the end, neither Shakuntala nor his mother left his side. In brief periods of lucidity between stretches of delirium, her husband held her hand and pressed it to his face: his eyes pleaded with his mother to look after her when he was gone. His mother's face turned stonier and stonier.

The good fortune that had marked Shakuntala's life like some charmed talisman came to an end with her husband's death. She was forced to stay with her husband's family, with her embittered and spiteful mother-in-law, and for the year that she remained with them, she lived in an earthly hell.

At first, Shakuntala had thought she might die from grief and did not know how she would live without the love and protection of her husband. Her grief was compounded by her ill treatment at the hands of her in-laws. She had gone from being adored to being reviled, looked upon as something filthy. Her head was shaved to remove the sin and pollution residing in her hair, and to mark her as the asexual being a widow had to be. She could still see the fury in her mother-in-law's eyes as she broke the glass bangles and ripped off the *mangal-sutra* from her neck in the first rites marking her passage into widowhood. She was stripped of all her jewellery and possessions and could cover her body with only a piece of white cloth; she was essentially slowly starved, as she was limited to one meal a day—and a meagre one of unseasoned rice and *daal* at that—to cleanse her body of lust. She had to sleep on the ground. Her only useful role, that of wife and producer of sons, was gone forever. She was not only viewed as responsible for her husband's death, but also as a threat to her husband's family and, most of all, to that of her dead husband's spirit, simply because of her vital womanhood and potential sexuality. She felt all eyes were constantly watching her, waiting for her to commit some sin that would bring curses on them and consign her husband to hell.

After a year, Shakuntala knew she had to leave. Her brothers made arrangements for her to go to the *ashram* in Rawalpur, and she would receive a small stipend every few months. Her parents had died, and Shakuntala blessed her brothers in her prayers. The money she received, and the fact that she could read and write with facility, gave her an independent position in the *ashram*. Her husband's family was happy to be rid of her, and she had had no contact with them in twelve years. Shakuntala had found a home in the *ashram* she would be loath to leave.

Chapter Sixteen

※

After a meagre dinner of rice and watery *daal*, Chuyia stole up the stairs to the *barsati*. She peered at the courtyard through the balcony railing to see if anyone was watching. Assured that no one had seen her, she crouched in front of Kalyani's locked door and looked through an opening where a panel had been removed.

The uneven tufts of dark hair framing her face, Kalyani sat, leaning against a wall. Her shorn head gave her beauty a fragile quality that stirred Chuyia's compassion. She spoke mournfully through the opening, "How will you get married now? You've become bald!"

Kalyani's lips twitched; she couldn't help smiling at this observation. "Don't worry. I'll get married," she assured Chuyia.

Chuyia, heartbroken at the cruel way Madhumati had treated her lovely friend, spat out, "I hope that fat Madhumati drowns!"

Later that afternoon, Chuyia slipped past Madhumati as she sat on her *takth*, waving her arms and haranguing the scandalized widows. "The Mahabharata says, 'Just as birds flock to a piece of flesh left on the ground, so all men try to seduce a widow.' Let's see how she gets married now! Shameless whore! If the child hadn't spoken, we'd all be contaminated by lustful sin."

Chuyia stealthily slipped into Madhumati's room. There was no one there except Mitthu. For a while, she stood there looking around, not sure what she could do to hurt the monstrous woman. She wanted to inflict a hurt as cruel as the one Madhumati had inflicted on Kalyani, as final as the way she had smashed Chuyia's own hopes. There was nothing of any worth she could destroy in the room. For a moment, she thought she would tear up her sheets, smash the hurricane lamp, overturn the small table and sweep everything on the shelves to the floor. But that wouldn't hurt the old devil enough. On an impulse, Chuyia moved quickly across the room and opened Mitthu's cage. The bird flapped a wing and began to squawk. As if in the grip of a nightmare she couldn't get out of, Chuyia plunged her hands in and grabbed the bird. Holding its wings still, she wrenched Mitthu out of the cage, and with a swift twist, wrung his neck.

Chuyia slowly became aware of the lifeless bird in her hands. Horrified at what she had done, she released Mitthu and he fell with a thud at her feet. She began to wretch and heave and threw up the little she had eaten that day.

Holding her hands out gingerly, as if they didn't belong to her and were mere appendages she was conveying elsewhere, Chuyia went straight to the well. She stood rubbing her hands with the rock-hard lump of soap that was there and poured water on them. She repeated the action several times. Not satisfied, she scraped up some dirt with her fingers and began scouring her hands with the mud.

Shakuntala, standing at her window, wondered what was taking Chuyia so long at the well. Her concern for the child made her sensitive to Chuyia's moods, and, feeling something was wrong, she went to her. "What are you doing!" she exclaimed taking Chuyia's raw hands in hers. She quickly rinsed them and pressed them in the folds of her sari to dry. Then, taking her little hands in hers, she led the child to her room.

≈

KALYANI PROSTRATED HERSELF on the dusty floor of the small *barsati* as she would before Krishna's statue. She swept her hand lightly over the dust and, getting up, touched her hands to her face. She shut her eyes tight, as was her wont, and prayed to Lord Krishna. She couldn't sleep. She went to the single barred window in the store-room and looked out, realizing she was imprisoned as much by culture and tradition as by the bars and locks on her room. She recognized the astonishing change that had taken place in her thinking since she had met Narayan, and the ways in which he had influenced her views. She wondered what he would do if he knew she was locked up, if he discovered how Madhumati had treated her.

She imagined Narayan storming into the *ashram*, giving a quaking Madhumati a learned tongue-lashing interspersed with Gandhi quotes, and, after breaking down the *barsati* door, leading her away through the ranks of the awestruck widows.

But this was a fantasy, far removed from reality. Kalyani knew the *ashram* was inviolate, and Madhumati's rule absolute. What happened in it was nobody's business but the *ashram*'s. Provided it adhered to its ordained rules and role, no one could interfere with its traditional governance and its sacrosanct place in society. Anyone who tried to defy the status quo would have to face the combined wrath of the religious and civil bastions of the city. Kalyani sank miserably to the floor and with the edge of her sari wiped the tears that rolled down her face. The moonlight shining through the warped slats in the wall fell across her in stripes.

GULABI STOOD AT MADHUMATI's window, slapping her forehead and ranting, "What a disaster! If one widow wants to marry, all the widows will want to marry. A calamity!"

Madhumati lay on her bed on her back, one hand flung dramatically over her brow, disinterested in Gulabi's rants.

Gulabi continued anyway. "Do you know what he says?"

"Who?" Madhumati responded half-heartedly.

"Gandhi. He says widows are strangers to love. And nobody should be a stranger to love!" When Madhumati did not respond to this earth-shaking charge, she continued. "Who loves me? Nobody! Why doesn't he say *hijras* are strangers to love? He should spare a thought or two of pity for us eunuchs."

Unexpectedly, Madhumati began to cry, softly at first. Gulabi looked at her in surprise. Had her eloquence moved her this much?

"What is it, *didi*?" Gulabi asked.

"I miss my Mitthu," wailed Madhumati. "My Mitthu. Where are you, my Mitthu?"

The old bitch couldn't care less for the plight of eunuchs! No one did, thought Gulabi.

Madhumati howled as if her heart were breaking into pieces. Gulabi began to cry for reasons that had nothing to do with dead parrots, and they bawled in a frightful chorus.

IN ONE OF THE WIDOW'S LARGER ROOMS, Kunti lay on a mat, head propped on her hand, gossiping with the other widows. "I hear someone twisted Mitthu's neck right off him, and left him on the floor," she whispered.

Kunti grew silent as Shakuntala walked through into an adjoining room where Chuyia lay on a mat. Shakuntala closed the door so that she and Chuyia would be left alone. She went to a corner and sat down close to Chuyia. Chuyia lay on her stomach with her face to the wall, seeming to sleep.

Shakuntala fetched a sari from her room and began to darn it, glancing at Chuyia every once in a while.

"Chuyia? Chuyia?" Shakuntala said, trying to see if she was awake. Something about the position in which she lay made her suspect she was.

Chuyia didn't answer, but Shakuntala noticed a slight tightening in her bare shoulders.

"I know you're not asleep," said Shakuntala.

Chuyia reluctantly rolled over to face Shakuntala. Her eyes were red and swollen.

"I won't ask about Mitthu," Shakuntala said. Then to show that she wouldn't, she changed the topic. She pushed her face forward. "Tell me, what do I look like?"

"Old!" answered Chuyia, matter-of-fact. Then she rolled back over, away from Shakuntala's eyes. How did she know about Mitthu? But it didn't matter if she knew. And as if she were relieved of a burden, Chuyia fell asleep.

Shakuntala sat, face impassive, and continued to darn.

Chapter Seventeen

⚍

A pale dawn light struggled through the overcast sky, and there was a rumble of approaching thunder. It started to drizzle as Shakuntala, sitting at the river's edge, filled the brass pot with water.

Sadananda sat high up on the *ghats*, slurping tea from a saucer under his mushroom-shaped umbrella. He idly watched Shakuntala fill the pot and walk up the *ghat* steps with the holy water. As the light shone through her damp sari, it outlined her thighs and legs. It gave him pleasure to watch her. Not for the first time, he observed the grace in her strong, shapely body. Her waist was slender above the rounded flare of her hips, her stomach flat. Her high breasts made shapely mounds beneath her handsome shoulders, and her neck sat straight above the indentations of her collarbones; he wished he could bury his lips in the hollows. He sighed. It was a pity she had become a widow while there was still so much life in her.

Shakuntala came up to him, and Sadananda could tell something was troubling her. Her brow was knit in a frown, and she avoided looking at him when she handed him the pot. Sadananda anointed her with the holy water and, after a brief glance of inquiry, sat back in his chair as Shakuntala set about preparing the place for worship. She would come out with whatever it was when it suited her.

As Shakuntala stood up from smoothing out his mat, her sari got pinched in the cleft between her buttocks. Sadananda had an almost irresistible urge to pry it out, and at the same time he feasted his eyes on the shape the round globes of her buttocks made. She turned to him, her eyes downcast, staring at nothing.

"Is something troubling you?" he asked, masking the desire in his voice and shading his eyes, as if from the glare, with his hand. Shakuntala sat down on the floor at his feet and, overcoming her hesitation and speaking gravely as was her wont, said, "Pandit*ji*, I have read the Holy Books without questioning them. But you have studied all the Holy Scriptures...I have great respect for your learning...Pandit*ji*, is it written that widows should be treated badly?"

Shakuntala was not given to saying much to him, and he was surprised by her loquacity and the almost provoking way she had phrased her question. He took a moment to consider the issue. Then he cleared his throat and gave her his considered answer in measured words:

"The Brahmanical tradition in the *stri-dharma* says a widow has two options: She can commit *sati* and mount her husband's pyre, or lead a life of self-denial and pray for her husband's soul. In some cases, if the family allows it, she may marry her dead husband's brother."

Shakuntala listened to him quietly. She already knew this: she had hoped his scholarship in religious matters had gleaned nuances of meaning not clear to a lay person like her. Disappointed, she unconsciously smoothed her sari at the back, and stood up to go. Sadananda stopped her with a gesture of his hand.

"However," he continued, "a law was recently passed which favours widow remarriage."

"A law?" Shakuntala said, surprised. "Why don't we know about it? Shouldn't we have been told?"

Sadananda gave a sardonic, lopsided grin and replied, "We ignore the laws that don't suit us."

Shakuntala stared at him, turning Sadananda's words over in her mind, allowing the truth of his statement to sink in: the law did not suit certain people in the *ashram*.

Shakuntala left the river and resolutely made her way to the *ashram*, mulling over the ramifications of the news she had just received. She was sickened at the thought of the deceit Madhumati had perpetrated on them all. She was infuriated by the image of the gullible widows gathered around her as she pontificated on the sins of widow-remarriage and the disaster she had saved them and the *ashram* from by discovering Kalyani's perfidy. Madhumati had deliberately withheld the information from Kalyani; she had no compunctions about destroying the young woman's only chance for happiness for selfish reasons. Who would support her dope addictions or some of the ease she enjoyed at the *ashram* if Gulabi stopped taking Kalyani to the *seths*? Kalyani raked in more money than the other widows she pimped out put together.

Shakuntala's sari was still damp from her dip in the river when she arrived at Madhumati's room. She leaned against the doorpost, observing Madhumati with the clear-eyed loathing of the betrayed, oblivious to the ringing of temple bells and the chirping of birds that filtered in from outside.

The object of her scrutiny stood before a small dresser topped by a tray filled with vials and pots of oils. She watched with revulsion as Madhumati dipped her fingers into a small pot and carefully traced the two-pronged ash caste-mark in the centre of her forehead. Madhumati daintily dabbed frankincense behind each earlobe with her little finger. The old woman noticed Shakuntala and turned to her with a slightly startled smile plastered to her face.

Without any trace of a returning smile to soften the severity of her features, Shakuntala said, "Give me the keys to Kalyani's room." Although she spoke quietly, the timbre of her voice was implacably determined.

Madhumati's smile vanished, and her face almost immediately hardened into a mask of anger. "Who do you think you are?" she growled. "I'm not giving you the keys."

Shakuntala stepped up to Madhumati until she was barely an inch from her face. "Give me the keys," she said with menacing resolve.

"No. Didn't you hear me?" Madhumati spat out the words. "I won't give them to you."

In a gesture that was almost violent, Shakuntala reached for the clump of keys knotted to Madhumati's sari and abruptly grabbed hold of them. Moving her lumpen arms with surprising agility, Madhumati clamped her hands on Shakuntala's. And as their eyes locked in a battle of wills, they grappled with the keys.

Shakuntala broke Madhumati's grip with a sharp tug. Unaccustomed to such open defiance, and stunned by shock, Madhumati stared as Shakuntala fell to her knees before her and with her teeth and fingers deftly pried open the knot that held the bunch of keys. Shakuntala walked from the room, and Madhumati bitterly called after her, "If you open that whore's door, you will destroy us all!"

Alerted by Madhumati's loud, distressed voice, the widows had grouped outside Madhumati's room and anxiously followed the altercation between them and the struggle for the keys. They broke rank to allow Shakuntala passage, and as she brushed past them Kunti placed a hand on Shakuntala's shoulder and pleaded, "Don't open the door, *didi*. Please, *didi*. Madhumati knows what's best for us."

Shakuntala pushed her hand off without deigning to respond and headed straight for the stairs leading to the *barsati*. For a moment, she stood nervously on the balcony outside the battered blue door. The uncertainty passed. She slipped the key into the lock, released the padlock and, sliding back the bolt, flung open the door.

Kalyani was slumped against the far wall nestling Kaalu in her lap. The room was dim, lit only by the slivers of light that came through the slits between the weathered boards of the walls. Her eyes were hollow, and her roughly shorn hair stuck out in a spiky halo around her head.

Silhouetted by the blinding daylight, Shakuntala stood in the door. "Leave. Go," she ordered, almost hissing with the tension coiled within her.

Kalyani was confused by the sudden visit. The unexpected command filled her with dread. Torn between the safety of the *barsati* and the freedom and danger that lay beyond the open door, she gaped at Shakuntala.

"What are you waiting for? Go. No one will stop you," Shakuntala said. "Don't worry. I'll send word to Narayan."

Holding onto Kaalu as if for support, Kalyani slowly got to her feet. She plucked a clean sari from a string stretched across the room and flung it over her bare shoulder. For a moment, she stood in front of Shakuntala, searching her face for answers. Shakuntala's strong face was unwavering, confidence-inspiring. She had learned to trust this woman. Marvelling at the resources of courage and strength the widow must have drawn upon to defy Madhumati and the tradition of the *ashram*, she quickly bent to touch Shakuntala's feet. As she straightened, the fear in her eyes was veiled by a glimmer of hope, of faint daring. With a look of mute appeal, she handed the puppy over to Shakuntala and walked out of the dark room and into the light.

Kaalu whimpered and squirmed on Shakuntala's shoulder. Her face reflected the concern she felt for Kalyani. Wondering how it would all end, she held Kaalu close and shut her eyes.

The agitated widows were lined up in the courtyard, waiting and watching, their awestruck faces grim with fear. Kunti stood with her wiry arms crossed in front of her, every muscle in her body tight with hostility towards Kalyani.

Her head and most of her face covered by the white sari, Kalyani walked through the wall of widows with slow, hesitant steps. Madhumati sat on her *takth*, staring bug-eyed, her lips flattened and drawn back, her head shaking with suppressed rage. As Kalyani passed, she raised a threatening finger. "Mind. If you go to him, I won't let you come back!"

The menace in her voice brought home the enormity of the risk she was about to take. After all, the *ashram* had sheltered her all these many years, even if it had made use of her body to procure income. God alone knew what would have happened to her without Madhumati's authority and Gulabi's vigil outside the doors of the strangers' houses. A hundred fears swirled through her mind. She looked back up to the balcony where Shakuntala stood, clutching Kaalu. Shakuntala gave her a small smile of encouragement and a nod to go on.

Kalyani continued her diffident walk toward the *ashram* exit much like a captive deer stepping out of its pen. Chuyia, who had been watching wide-eyed from behind a pillar, popped out for a moment, then jumped back into hiding as Kalyani passed.

Kalyani traced her accustomed route to the river. She sat down on the grey stone steps of Shiva's Temple at Karmi Ghat, collecting her incoherent thoughts and grounding herself in the reality of the events that had so recently overtaken her life and turned it upside down, and would from now on define it. After a while, she splashed water onto her face. The sun was high, and the sky and water were a matching pale blue. Bathed in sunlight and warmed by it, Kalyani soaped and washed her hair and body in the gentle flow of the river, and cleansed her limbs of the accumulated grime of her incarceration in the *barsati*. Behind her, a middle-aged widow was sprinkling holy water on a white statue of a cow. On the far side of the river, the densely green and lush foliage enclosed a mysterious world she had never ventured into.

Revived by her bath, Kalyani made her way to the majestic banyan near the river where she had had her first assignation with Narayan. She didn't know where else to go. If Shakuntala's message had reached Narayan, this is where he would expect to find her. Pulling her sari forward over her face, she sat down, head bowed, on the stone parapet, a forlorn figure beneath the overarching branches of the mighty tree.

What if Narayan was out of town and didn't receive Shakuntala's message? What if he didn't show up? Kalyani's hands appeared to have acquired a will of their own as they clasped each other nervously in her lap. She stared at the unwilled movements of her hands and at her bare feet. Kalyani was thankful there were very few people around, but, bereft of Narayan's presence, the calm of the landscape offered little comfort. Although there was shade beneath the tree, beyond its sheltering reach, the daylight was stark and terrible.

"Kalyani!" a voice called from behind her. It was Narayan. Kalyani's heart lurched, and all her senses came alive. By the time she turned to him, her face was transformed with relief, radiant with joy. Throwing her habitual widow's decorum and caution to the wind, she rushed across the distance that separated them and fell into Narayan's outstretched arms. For a moment, he clasped her to him hard, nuzzling her neck. Her movements were uninhibited and spontaneous for the first time since Narayan had known her; and it was the first time that Narayan had held her so close. His body was filled with rapture as it responded to the softness of her. She felt fragile against him, like a dove, and he loosened his grip, afraid of hurting her. After a while, he held her away from him so he could look at her. His eyes became troubled as he searched her face. He was shocked to see the change wrought on her in the few days since he'd last seen her. He had learned of her ordeal only from the note Shakuntala had sent him. He thought he'd go mad when he heard that Madhumati had cut Kalyani's hair and locked her in the *barsati*, and his heart ached with helpless fury at the harsh words Madhumati must have spoken while committing these atrocities and the threats she must have hurled. Shakuntala's brief note had only mentioned that Madhumati had warned that Kalyani would not be allowed back into the *ashram*.

Narayan ran his hands over Kalyani's cropped hair, as if to examine the wounds afflicted on the hair and heal the damage done to her. He pulled her close to him again, and his hands wandered over her bare shoulders and neck. He had never felt her like this before, and the silken texture of her skin and her firm flesh was almost like a shock that broke in waves of desire all over him. "I love you very much," he said, almost weeping from the accumulated tension of desire and of tenderness for her suffering. He felt the softness of her breasts pressing against him, and, his fingers trembling, he gently pressed her breasts under the sari. They seemed to bloom in his hands as Kalyani yielded her body to his touch.

After a while, Narayan, frightened at the way their bodies were responding, pulled back a little. What if somebody were observing them? It would not be good for Kalyani. He would have to look out for her. Kalyani looked at him, startled, her desiring eyes locked on his with naked pleading. Overwhelmed by the thought of how much she meant to him, he felt his whole being dissolve and be absorbed into those tawny eyes, while her entire body trembled in his arms. For a while, he lost all control over his will.

Then, with a monumental effort, he held her away. "We have the rest of our lives to love each other," he said, stroking a short wisp of hair back from her forehead. "Will you marry me?" he asked.

The hurt that had clouded Kalyani's face at being so suddenly separated from his body dissolved. Her eyes shone with love. She nodded almost imperceptibly, and, sliding her eyes away, bent down to touch his feet. She resisted his pressure to raise her up and swept her hand lightly over the dirt as she was used to before Krishna's statue. She let him pull her up. She brushed her hand over her face and lips, embracing the dust he had trod upon. Narayan held her in a close embrace. "I love you so much. I will never let you go," he said, as bits of sunlight sparkled through gaps in the tree's leaves and danced upon them.

Chapter Eighteen

≈

The sounds of celebration, accompanied by the pounding of dual-ended *dholak* drums, rang out around Chuyia. The smoky smell of incense hung in the air as wisps of smoke and coloured dust-motes swirled about the women. Chuyia was decked out as a little Krishna by the adoring widows for Holi, the Festival of Colour. Her forehead had been decorated with a yellow "V," and her eyes and brows outlined by a series of white dots. The striped blue-and-yellow scarf tied around her head like a turban gave her an air of rakish exuberance, which was a bit at odds with the sadness in her eyes. She missed Kalyani.

Chuyia heard Shakuntala calling for her, and then Shakuntala was kneeling in front of her with a tray full of coloured powders. She grabbed a fistful of gaudy pink and applied swaths of it on Chuyia's cheeks and chin. It was as if she were determined to draw a clown's cheerful smile on the young girl's face. Chuyia looked like a joker. Succumbing to Shakuntala's ministrations and the joyful atmosphere around them, Chuyia was beaming by the time Shakuntala was done with her. Then it was Chuyia's turn to decorate Shakuntala, which she did with an exuberant application of colour to her face. Shakuntala took Chuyia by the hand and led her to the centre of the courtyard to take her place in the throng of dancing widows.

Shedding petals from the thick garland of pink-and-white flowers that swung from her neck and the miniature garlands that circled her arms and ankles, Chuyia danced with the widows. The shorn women carried platters filled with colours and painted the air with clouds of powder as they lumbered about awkwardly, their faces, feet and saris a bizarre montage from the many hues flung into the air. It looked as if the ground itself had turned ochre from the sloping rays of the sun.

Chuyia took the wooden flute given to her by Shakuntala and carefully held it sideways, flush to her lips. Her elbows stuck out as she placed one foot on her knee and, standing on one foot, adopted the stylized posture of Krishna's statues. Playing out her role as Lord Krishna incarnate, she hopped in the circle formed by the widows and then, dancing up to them, romanced each in turn. Even Kunti had a smile on her face.

Chuyia stole away from the group and approached Madhumati, who was sitting to one side on her *takth* watching the widows frolic with a proprietary and benevolent air. The old woman's eyes sparkled with merriment as she smiled at Chuyia. Chuyia chose the same shocking-pink Shakuntala had applied to her face and cheekily rubbed it all over Madhumati's face before darting off. Madhumati's head wobbled on the folds of her wattled neck as she swayed beatifically and clapped in time to the music.

THE SOUNDS OF THE *dholak* drums and of firecrackers popping travelled across the calm waters of the grey-brown Ganga to Kalyani and Narayan in their small boat. They were headed upstream toward the main *ghats* of the city. Kalyani sat behind the oarsman, facing Narayan. A gentle breeze stirred in her hair and blew wisps into her face. After a while, she wet her hand and ran it over the unruly tufts of her badly cut hair to smooth it down.

"Don't do that," Narayan said. "You look even more beautiful with your hair mussed up."

Kalyani smiled and, looking at Narayan out of the corner of her eyes, slowly ran her fingers through her hair so that it lifted off her head and shook the uneven tufts free. Narayan could not take his eyes off her. She looked radiant, content; and as a bud touched by the sun blooms, she flowered in the caress of his gaze. "Don't look at me all the time. It makes me shy," she said, discomfited by his gaze.

Narayan turned his head away slightly and removed his dreamy eyes to the horizon, to the pink clouds banked against the deepening-blue evening sky.

But outside the orbit of his adoring gaze, Kalyani wilted. "No, look at me," she said, reaching out to touch his face. "I'm prettier than the clouds."

"You are," Narayan agreed, charmed by the change in her. Already her diffidence was being replaced by a winsome confidence. Then, pretending to mull over the question, he teased, "But are you as lovely as the full moon?"

"Don't compare me to the moon by daylight," Kalyani said. "Wait till it's out at night—then tell which is lovelier."

"I wouldn't see the moon if you are there," Narayan said, taking her hands in his own and discreetly kissing her fingers. After a while, he touched the coarse material of her sari. "You don't need to wear white all the time."

Kalyani looked startled. "I have only these white saris," she said. She ran her hand over the sari she had folded and placed by her side; it was still damp.

"It is Holi today, the Festival of Colour," declared Narayan.

"I know," Kalyani said. "Chuyia will have become Krishna today," she said wistfully.

"You are very attached to her, aren't you?" Narayan said, looking at her thoughtfully. "We will adopt her, bring her and Kaalu to our house." He added, "If you wish."

Kalyani lowered her lids. Her heart leapt up as if it were Kaalu jumping up to lick her throat. "I wish it very much," she said, speaking so softly that only a lover's keen ears could have picked up her words.

"It's settled then," Narayan said, touching her chin to tilt up her face. "I'm very fond of her too," he said gently, and Kalyani knew he meant it. Her face lit up. Narayan shimmered before her like an avatar through the sudden tears of joy that welled in her eyes.

"Hey, what's this?" said Narayan, holding her face and brushing her tears with his thumbs. The tears and the evening light had turned her eyes molten. He felt humbled by her happiness.

Kalyani was unable to speak.

"Let's talk about you," Narayan said, his voice husky with emotion. "Tell me. What is the first colour you'd like to wear?"

Kalyani sat back and, composing herself, gave the question the attention it merited. "Blue?" she said, tentatively. "Yes, blue. The colour of Krishna," she said.

"I'll tell Ma to buy you a blue silk sari with a gold border to match your eyes. You'll look as splendid as a peacock's feather in it," said Narayan, smiling.

Kalyani's demeanour changed. "You really told your mother about me?" she asked timidly, not quite believing he had actually dared to.

"Yes," Narayan answered simply and truthfully.

"What did you say?" Kalyani asked shyly.

"I said I wanted to marry you."

"And what did she say?"

Narayan smiled, recalling the scene with his mother. "She began to cry," he answered honestly.

Kalyani was dismayed. "*Hai Ram!*" she said, and buried her face in her hands.

Narayan laughed and pried her hands away. "Don't worry. Father and I will bring her around. We'll convince her you are the best daughter-in-law she can wish for."

There were more boats on the river now, some larger craft with groups of merrymakers showering each other with clouds of colour, and other skiffs like theirs with two or three people enjoying an evening outing. As the sun sank lower into the clouds, a few boats skimmed past them at more purposeful speeds, conveying mourners and their dead to or from the *ghats*. A shrouded form she glimpsed reminded Kalyani of Bua, the poor old woman who had died in their midst, and a stab of anger and sadness shot through her, dispelling her euphoria. Surely Madhumati could have sent for a doctor to ease her last moments.

But mostly these crafts drifted at the edges of the river, artfully silhouetted against the burning pyres and the glow from the setting sun.

As the boat took a bend in the river, a bulky white mansion, with turrets and bulging towers and haphazardly tacked-on extensions that reflected different architectural eras, rose like an ungainly galleon from a bed of rock and trees at some distance behind Kalyani. "Look—that's my house," Narayan said, gesturing toward the mansion.

Kalyani turned around to look at the building Narayan was pointing out. An ominous chill coursed through her blood and drained the colour from her face. Kalyani turned her eyes to Narayan and in a deathly quiet voice she asked, "What is your father's name?"

"Dwarkanath...Seth Dwarkanath."

The blood chilled to ice in Kalyani's veins and turned her body numb. Dark blotches swam before her eyes, blocking out huge portions of the bloated building. The river appeared to heave, and she thought she would pass out. With a monumental effort, she willed herself to remain conscious. Eyes downcast, her voice low, she commanded, "Turn the boat around."

"Why? What happened?" asked Narayan, baffled by the sudden change in her mood. He noticed her pallor and the tautness around her mouth and eyes. He thought the motion of the boat was making her queasy. "Are you feeling sick?" he asked.

"Turn the boat around," Kalyani repeated more forcefully.

There was terror in her stricken face. She began to

stand up, and as the boat rocked from side to side Narayan sensed she would rather jump into the water and swim back than let the boat take her forward.

"Sit down, Kalyani," he ordered, wondering what had caused this reaction. Grasping her by her shoulders, he tried to steady her. The boatman called a warning and gestured to them to sit down. Glancing over his shoulder, Narayan shouted: "Turn the boat around, *bhaiya*." The boat wobbled perilously and, losing their balance, they abruptly thudded down on the hard seats.

"At least tell me what's wrong," Narayan said, once the boat's movement had stabilized. His face was ashen, his eyes pleading.

Kalyani remained silent, resolute. The boat, making a wide arc, slowly turned direction and brought her face to face with her nemesis.

"All right; you don't need to say anything," Narayan said, not wanting to upset her further, confident she would tell him when she was ready to.

"But I do need to..." Kalyani said, and abruptly broke off mid-sentence. Torn between the need to make him understand why she had to turn back and not wanting to reveal the ugly truth, she was at a loss.

"Then please try," said Narayan

"I can't..." she said. Then, looking desperately at him, Kalyani gave him as much of an answer as she could. "Ask your father," she said simply.

"What?" Mystified, Narayan could not imagine what his father had to do with Kalyani's determination to turn back. As a glimmer of comprehension dawned at the edges of his mind, he was overcome by a deep foreboding. His throat constricted and then swelled. He shifted on the plank and, leaning over the edge of the boat, threw up.

≋

SADHURAM KNOCKED DISCREETLY on the door to Seth Dwarkanath's room. He could hear muffled voices speaking inside.

"Come in!" The Seth's usually genial tone was uncommonly gruff.

Sadhuram entered unobtrusively. Their conversation had stalled; Chhotay Babu stood by the window staring stonily into the night. Seth Dwarkanath sat awkwardly on the edge of his bed, abstractedly puffing on his hookah. His grey, henna-streaked hair fell in lank strands about his face, and his beard was grizzled and unkempt. Something was seriously amiss between father and son. Sadhuram placed the lit oil lamp and a salver with two glasses of water on a small table between the two beds and quietly withdrew.

After the servant left, Dwarkanath took a sip of water from the glass. His eyes, restless beneath his hooded lids, belied his calm. "What happened was unfortunate, son.... However..." He stopped short as Narayan whipped around and turned on him angrily.

"However, *what?*" Narayan prompted with barely contained contempt. He strode from the window and sat down on the bed across from his father.

Dwarkanath sighed and laid his hookah to one side. His belly bulged under his white *kurta*, and he felt disad-

200

vantaged in his uncomfortable posture. Narayan had burst in on him with questions and accusations, and hadn't given him the time to compose himself. "I'm sorry you are disillusioned, son," he said, speaking kindly and with as much dignity as he could muster under the circumstances. "But you cannot go through life being so idealistic." Turning his palms out to indicate that the situation was not as serious as Narayan believed it was, he said, "So you've found out she's not a goddess. Don't marry her—keep her as your mistress."

Narayan looked at his father in disbelief. He got up and took a step forward to loom threateningly over him. "I respected you so much," he said bitterly.

Dwarkanath navigated his feet into his slippers and also stood up. He had not expected his words to wound his son so deeply. He should be more careful. He had forgotten what it was to be so young and so hot-blooded. He placed a placating hand on the young man's shoulder. "Narayan, perhaps you are not aware of this. Our Holy Texts say Brahmins can sleep with whomever they want, and the women they sleep with are blessed."

Narayan's face was a dark cloud of confusion and incredulity. He tore his father's hand from his shoulder. "I have also studied our scriptures," he said, breathing heavily and struggling to retain some control over his voice. "God Ram told his brother never to honour those Brahmins who interpret the Holy Texts for their own benefit."

"You're not a hero in some mythic play, ready to embrace martyrdom," said Dwarkanath, averting his eyes from his son.

Narayan slowly backed away. "You disgust me," he said, his voice heavy with loathing and disappointment. He turned his broad back on his father and stalked from the room.

Narayan's mother stood just outside the door. Her face was ravaged. *She must have heard every word of the heated exchange*, thought Narayan, as he stopped and turned to her. *She must have known of his tawdry infidelities: how could she tolerate them?* He knew at the same time that she had no options but to. It was not such a rare transgression, in fact, as Rabindra had pointed out; the Seths of Rawalpur seemed to fancy widows. He looked at his mother with compassion. Bhagwati reached up and gently held her son's face in both her hands. Her eyes were brimming with sympathy and understanding as she gazed at him. She smiled through her tears and tenderly ran her hands over his hair, his face. Without uttering a word she brought his head forward and pressed her lips to his forehead. With these silent gestures, she let Narayan know that he had her blessing to follow his heart. At last she released him, and as he left her face crumpled in despair.

∾

KALYANI SAT ON THE GRAVEL in the dark alley outside Madhumati's room, her back against the wall. The warm night was humid and the stillness oppressive. Madhumati had told her she could never come back to the *ashram*— but there was nowhere else for her to go. The only light came from a single candle that flickered in Madhumati's room and shone faintly through the barred window.

Kalyani got to her feet slowly. She looked shrunken, as if the loss of hope were a physical thing and had diminished her flesh. She picked distractedly at the threads on the edge of her sari as she tried to summon the courage to speak to Madhumati. Her dreams and hopes of a future with Narayan had been blasted in one revealing instant, and the destructive potential of that horrific instant was still filtering in, weighing her down with the realization of all that she had lost and the precarious position she was in. With every passing moment, a new tormenting thought struck her, and she flagellated herself with blame. How could she have ever imagined she would marry Narayan? Live happily ever after with him? It was a children's fairy tale: something Chuyia could have been expected to dream up. She should have known better, kept her distance from Narayan. For all his book learning and appreciation of poems, he was simple; he didn't know of the deeply entrenched stranglehold of tradition. She knew. She should have protected him. Had she seduced him with languishing looks, small flirtations? She should not have allowed herself to fall in love with him, and let him fall so hard for her. Would he still want to marry her now that he'd had more time to mull over the matter? She suspected he would. But she knew she would never be able to face Seth Dwarkanath no matter what. Nor could she saddle Narayan's noble family with a daughter-in-law whose every living moment would bring disgrace and dishonour to their house. By now they must know the entire sordid story; Narayan was sure to have confronted his father. What must they think of her? What contempt, what loathing, would the Seth have for her? What must his

mother think of her? The thought was unbearable. Filled
with self-loathing, she cringed in terror against the wall.

Kunti came in the room carrying a steel *thali* laden
with food for Madhumati. "Did you add the butter?"
Madhumati demanded, sitting up on her bed and leaning against the wall to receive the platter.

"Yes," Kunti nodded and, picking up an empty steel
glass with a residue of milk sticking to the rim, left.

Kalyani stood outside the window watching
Madhumati eat. She ate with gusto, making loud smack-
ing sounds. Kalyani finally gathered up the courage.
"*Didi*?" she said hesitantly.

Surprised to hear Kalyani's voice, Madhumati
turned toward the window. Her eyes flickered across
Kalyani's pallid face. The play of shadows cast by the
bars made her look as if she were peering out of a cage—
Mitthu's cage. Madhumati very deliberately turned away
and continued eating.

A little later she said, "So, you've come back. Your
father-in-law didn't like you?" she asked cruelly, between
bites. She gave Kalyani a long look. "He could have had
you for free."

Kalyani didn't answer.

Relishing her power over Kalyani and gloating over
her return, Madhumati matter-of-factly said, "Wait
there. Gulabi will be here soon."

Had she expected some consideration from
Madhumati? Some sort of healing shelter in which to lick
her wounds before she could decide what to do? Despite
knowing her as well as she did, she stupidly had. Kalyani
stood in the alley, staring into the dark. Nothing had

changed. And yet everything had. Her breathing was rapid and shallow. She was like an animal caught in a snare.

Madhumati kept stuffing food into her mouth. When she turned to the window again, Kalyani was gone.

Kalyani knew she had no choice: there was only one avenue open to her. Cast out in the streets she would die, but to live without Narayan and return to a life of forced prostitution would be a worse kind of death. Her very existence would cast a shadow on Narayan's life and blight it.

Kalyani dragged herself listlessly through the dark alleys to the *ghats*. There was hardly anyone about, only a few ghostly shadows like herself. She went down the steep stone stairs and stood on the last step, where the river lapped gently at its edge. The funeral pyres burned steadily behind her. Kalyani carefully folded the extra sari she had been carrying with her and set it down on a dry slab. She took one step into the shallow water at the river's edge and then sat down on the last stair. The cool water seeped through her sari, but her body was so cold that it felt warm against her skin. She removed a brown cloth-band from her wrist, and set it gently on top of the folded sari. Kalyani rose and walked slowly into the river until the water came up to her knees. She bent to splash her face with the sacred water that flowed from Shiva's head, and smoothed it over her face and hair. She clasped her hands in prayer for a moment. Then she calmly walked into the river until her short hair floated in an inky stain on the water.

Ma Ganga had claimed her daughter.

Chapter Nineteen

≈

There was a loud, persistent knocking on the heavy wooden door of the *ashram*. Shakuntala, awakened from a fitful sleep, slowly shuffled toward the door in the faint light at the edge of dawn. She drew back the small panel in the top of the door and peered out.

Narayan stood on the other side. He was unshaven, his *kurta* and *dhoti* rumpled, but his eyes were calm. A suitcase stood at his feet.

Narayan saw Shakuntala's pale, staring face in the opening and said simply, "I've come for Kalyani."

Shakuntala's stricken features filled with sorrow and sympathy. She would have to find the words to tell Narayan that he was too late.

≈

THE DAY OF KALYANI'S CREMATION was like any other sultry day. The dawn clouds had been dispersed by the sun that was already quite high. Narayan stood against a brick wall that ran along the *ghat*, unable to take his eyes away from Kalyani's pyre. After a while, he walked down the steps to join Shakuntala and Chuyia, who sat close together lower down the *ghat*. Her small white sari covering her from head to toe, Chuyia gnawed on her knuckles, fretful and restless, wiping her nose on her sari and every short while brushing tears that welled up in her eyes when she realized she would never see her friend again. Narayan sat down next to them quietly and stared off across the river. He wasn't wearing his glasses, as if he didn't want his vision sharpened on this day; the reality of what had happened, the blaze of the consuming pyre, were all too vividly lodged in his heart.

Shakuntala turned her head to look at Narayan. He wore a long, pale blue shirt over a white *dhoti*. His feet were bare. The boyish contours of his face had acquired a discernible hardness that made him appear older than his twenty-two years. Why should he not have changed after what had happened? She sat with her hands folded in her lap, looking at him. He could feel her sad eyes on him, and he was comforted by her presence. He did not feel the need to speak. In an attempt to draw him out and to offer consolation, Shakuntala, after a while, said, "The Holy Texts tell us that all this is *maya*, an illusion."

"Kalyani's death is no illusion," Narayan said, the peremptory tone and his gruff voice expressing some of the anger coiled within him.

Shakuntala was shocked by Narayan's explicit denigration of the Holy Books. She moved closer to him. "Narayan, no matter what happens, you must not lose faith," she said, laying her hand on his shoulder and thinking of how much comfort those words uttered by Sadananda had given her.

Narayan did not look at her. "Why is your faith so strong?" he challenged.

Shakuntala was stunned by the question, disturbed by the cynicism that laced his voice. "I don't know," was her honest reply.

Chuyia stood up and listlessly wandered off. Shakuntala watched her go, a worried frown creasing her forehead. Narayan noticed the direction of her gaze, and his features softened. The hubbub of an ordinary day on the river continued all around them. A body wrapped in white and tied to the litter at the ankles and neck lay on the steps next to them, the heels barely clearing the water. Behind them, the funeral pyres burned in anemic heaps, their lustre overpowered by the greater fire of the sun. A little way off, a man was getting his head shaved on the *ghat* steps. Life continued in the face of death.

"There must be a reason for it. Why are we sent here?" Shakuntala said, continuing her train of thought as she spoke to Narayan, still trying to grasp for some meaning in the futile loss of Kalyani's young life that might offer them both consolation.

"One less mouth to feed, four saris, one bed to let—somewhere a corner saved for another widow. There is no other reason. Disguised as religion, it's just about money."

His severe assessment had the ring of truth; Shakuntala was surprised that she thought so. Narayan stood up to leave, pausing for a moment to stare at Kalyani's pyre. His gait, as he climbed up the steps, was weary, his tread heavy. As he dissolved into the crowd,

Shakuntala wondered at the meaning of Kalyani's life, at the unfairness that had stamped its short span—at the promise of happiness that had fallen into her lap like a ripe fruit she could never partake of.

LATER THAT DAY, MADHUMATI sat on her bed leaning against the wall, her short legs stretched out in front like loaves of dough beneath her sari. She picked at her ear with a wooden matchstick, grimacing at the wax she excavated. Gulabi leaned forward, pressed up against the window bars, stuffing the small aperture with her gaudy colours.

Chuyia, having been summoned by Madhumati, stood uneasily in the doorway.

Madhumati assumed an impish air of childish animation, and began laying the groundwork for her new plan to finance the *ashram* and her addictions. "I always keep my promises," she stated, turning to Gulabi for confirmation. "Don't I?"

Gulabi nodded her head obligingly. "Everyone knows you do," she concurred, removing the dirt from under her nails with a matchstick.

Turning to Chuyia, Madhumati continued in the same playful vein, "But she doesn't even want to go home. Right?"

Chuyia, wanting desperately to believe that Madhumati truly would send her home, but full of misgiving, said in a small voice, "I want to go home."

"Alright then, Gulabi will take you," Madhumati said with a flick of her hand, as if what she promised were of no great moment and could easily be conjured up.

Chuyia, whose wishes had been so consistently thwarted that she had stopped thinking of home, looked at her, clearly puzzled. "You know where my house is?"

"She does," Madhumati said, flicking her thumb at Gulabi. "Gulabi knows everything. But if you don't want to go, you don't have to," she said, simpering coyly. "After all, I'm also like your mother, aren't I?" Madhumati batted her eyelids and directed a smile of such saccharine sweetness at Chuyia that it set even Gulabi's teeth on edge.

Like her mother? Chuyia was appalled at the idea. She nervously fingered the sari edge that was biting into her shoulder. After a moment she ventured tentatively, "Can I take Kaalu?"

Madhumati's face lit up in a bright munificent smile by way of answer and at the same time she gave Gulabi a knowing look. Gulabi raised her eyes from her grimy nails and looked at Chuyia. Chuyia was staring at her expectantly. Gulabi's lips stretched in a toothy, betel nut-stained smile. "Come, I'll take you," she said, with an indifferent toss of her elaborately coifed head.

While Madhumati and Gulabi were talking to Chuyia at the *ashram*, Shakuntala was saying her final goodbyes to Kalyani. She sat on her heels at the river's edge and released Kalyani's ashes, using her hands as paddles to maneuver them away from the shore. They floated away in a red-glazed pot covered with a green cloth.

Sadananda stood behind Shakuntala, his eyes shut and hands clasped, offering prayers for Kalyani's soul in a sonorous chant. "O Spirit of the Dead! Carry with you only the good karmas! Seek a new body! And a life of glory!" He turned to Shakuntala. "Holy water...."

Shakuntala appeared not to hear him. Even after the pot sailed away, Shakuntala stayed crouched, her empty arms turned outwards and stretched towards the disappearing ashes. The bottom of her sari was getting wet from the puddles on the step, but she didn't notice.

The priest gently urged Shakuntala to get up and follow him. Her ability to respond seemed to have slowed. After a while, she stood up and they started the walk to Tulsi Ghat. The bottle palms swayed gently in the breeze. A group of muscle-bound wrestlers, oil gleaming on their bare skin, chanted as they marched past the pair.

All at once the calm of the late afternoon was broken by a young man rushing through the crowded *ghats*, distributing pamphlets and shouting, "The British have let Gandhi*ji* out of jail! He's free!" He thrust a pamphlet at Shakuntala and she took it. "His train will stop here on his way from Allahabad," he shouted, as if directing the message at the woman and the priest. The young man continued yelling the news of Gandhi's arrival down the length of the *ghats*, too excited to have any qualms about disrupting the prayers of the pious.

Sadananda's mouth twisted into a sad, wry smile. "Gandhi is one of the few people in the world who listens to the voice of his conscience."

"But what if our conscience conflicts with our faith?" asked Shakuntala, finally articulating the question that had been tormenting her all day.

Chapter Twenty

≈

The sun had set, and in its picturesque afterglow Gulabi steered the boat to the private dock of Seth Bhupindernath's mansion in Hajipur, on the outskirts of Rawalpur. She helped Chuyia out of the boat and, holding her by her hand, led her up the tall flight of steps to the mansion looming above them. Chuyia stopped short of the entryway. Still out of breath from her climb, she gaped at the bulky structure. Up close, it looked decayed and menacing: the kind of palace that locked up princesses in dungeons. "Whose house is this?" she asked Gulabi, nervously twisting the edge of her sari.

"This is Kalyani's friend's house. You can play here for a while. Then I'll take you home," said Gulabi glibly.

Gulabi's facile tone of voice alarmed Chuyia as much as the ugly mansion. She stubbornly refused to move. "No," she told Gulabi. "I don't want to play here."

"Huh? Don't you want sweets and fried bread?" said Gulabi.

"Where is Kalyani's friend? Tell her to come out." Chuyia said, balking at the thought of entering this forbidding house.

"Upstairs, in the house," said Gulabi, casually shrugging her shoulders. "Don't you want to eat *laddoos* and cake?"

Chuyia considered this. It was getting late and she was hungry. Her face brightened at the prospect of savouring these forbidden treats.

"Let's go," Gulabi said, firmly taking her by the hand and leading her to that same back verandah that Kalyani had reluctantly traversed so many times. They passed the mildewing, flaking pillars in the neglected rear of the mansion, and walked through a flock of hens pecking at crumbs on the floor. Chuyia, succumbing to the lure of this new adventure, looked around her curiously, her spirits still buoyed in anticipation of the promised sweets to come. Somewhere inside the dark house, a clock chimed. They arrived at the metal service staircase. Chuyia followed Gulabi unhesitatingly up the spiral stairs.

Gulabi stepped through a lace-curtained doorway, gently pushing Chuyia ahead of her. She gave a slight nod to a shadowy figure ensconced in an elaborate, four-poster bed. Shaking her hand free of Chuyia's tightening grip, she quickly exited and shut the door behind her. Chuyia was suddenly alone. Her eyes darted to the panels of the tall door through which Gulabi had just disappeared. Her small heart pounding, she turned fearfully toward the room. As she tugged at her sari, she became aware of the music coming from the large, ear-shaped horn of a gramophone. Where was Kalyani's friend? The room was dark, filled with heavy mahogany furniture. The walls were painted blue. There was a reddish glow to the room; it came from a red glass lamp that stood on a table next to the bed. As her eyes adjusted to the dim light, Chuyia could just make out the shape of a man leaning back against the cushions, drink in hand, puffing on a hookah. His face was obscured by the canopy of mosquito netting, which hung over the bed. He didn't speak, so she introduced herself.

"My name is Chuyia. I've come to play."

※

IT WAS NIGHT IN THE *ashram* courtyard. Snehlata lit incense at the stone altar on which a *pradip* already burned. Grim-faced and troubled, she knelt before it to pray. Shakuntala came into the courtyard, calling for Chuyia. The elderly widow gave her a tentative, sidelong look, but did not say anything, as Shakuntala rushed past her to look into the widows' room and the kitchen; she finally ran up the stairs to the *barsati*. Finding no trace of the girl, she came back down to the courtyard and confronted the woman directly. "Have you seen Chuyia?"

Too afraid and wretched to reveal the truth of Chuyia's whereabouts, the widow remained ominously quiet. When Shakuntala stepped closer, she turned her stern, lantern-like face to her and told her, "Ask Madhu-*didi*."

A stab of fear shivered through Shakuntala. She raced to Madhumati's room. Madhumati lay in a deep stupor, her face slack, a circle of drool on her pillow. The sounds of dogs barking in the distance and of crickets chirping filtered in through the closed window.

Shakuntala shook Madhumati's shoulder and demanded, "Where's Chuyia? Have you seen Chuyia?" Her voice was hoarse with fear.

Madhumati did not respond. Shakuntala shook her slack body harder.

"What?" Madhumati slurred the word, barely able to move her heavy lids.

"Have you seen Chuyia?" shouted Shakuntala, growing more frantic by the second.

Madhumati's eyes snapped open. She gave Shakuntala a dreamy smile of recognition and fell back asleep.

Her lips drawn back in an angry snarl, Shakuntala placed both her hands firmly on Madhumati's ears and shook her head hard enough to make her teeth rattle. "Have you seen Chuyia!" she screamed, desperation making her voice crack.

Madhumati opened her drugged eyes with difficulty. They were bloodshot, and the pupils were dilated. "I've sent her." Her speech was slurred, and the words dribbling from her mouth ended on a note of finality that chilled her heart.

Shakuntala wouldn't stop shaking her. "Where did you send her? Where did you send her? OPEN YOUR EYES! WHERE DID YOU SEND HER!" she shrieked.

Unable to struggle out of her stupor, Madhumati started to whimper in fear. "With Gulabi," she mumbled. "Gulabi has..."

Shakuntala slapped Madhumati hard across the face. The old woman's head shook from the force of the blow, but she didn't awaken. Clamping her clenched fist to her mouth, Shakuntala fled from the room.

Shakuntala ran blindly through the dark gullies. The distant roar of chants came at her in waves from Tulsi Ghat. Although she could not make out the words, she knew what they were. Once she arrived at the *ghats* the words, rising from a thousand throats, resounded all around her. "*Ram Nam Satya Hai*—Ram, Thy Name is Truth," chanted the mourners, heightening her sense of urgency, and she rushed down the steps to the river. Shakuntala awoke one boatman after another, pleading desperately with each in turn to take her up the river to Hajipur. None of the exhausted men were willing to go. Their long shifts over, they were done for the day.

Suddenly, Shakuntala spotted a boat with an odd splash of colour bobbing in it. As the boat moved toward the bank, the colours, in the flicker of lights from the *ghat*, became more vivid. Who but Gulabi would dress in blues and reds so flamboyant? Shakuntala ran along the embankment, keeping abreast of the boat. Gulabi's belly protruded beneath her short blouse and hung over her scarlet sari as she rowed toward the bank with long, powerful strokes. Shakuntala could just make out a small, crumpled form lying in a heap in the front of the boat. She shouted incoherently at Gulabi. Gulabi, who never lacked the instinct of self-preservation, quickly took in the situation. Shakuntala's rage was palpable. Like a mother bear whose cub is endangered, she was quite liable to bound into the boat and thrash the life out of her. Before the boat could come to a stop, Gulabi leaped onto the embankment and, grunting in fear, fled flat-footed past Shakuntala.

Shakuntala stepped into the boat. She knelt down beside Chuyia's curled body and, speaking softly, lifted the little girl's chin with the tips of her fingers to look into her eyes. "Open your eyes, Chuyia," Shakuntala pleaded. "Try…Try to open them." Chuyia's eyebrows twitched and, as her head fell back, white moons showed beneath the fringe of her lashes. Shakuntala grew rigid with fear and fury. Chuyia had been drugged. What had the beast done to a drugged child? Shakuntala struggled to pick up the inert body and, with great difficulty, hauled Chuyia onto the embankment. For a long while, she sat on the *ghat* steps, holding Chuyia close to her heart and rocking her gently. She drifted in and out of sleep with the child in her arms, and when she half-awakened to a clamour of temple bells, she guessed it must be well past midnight.

Dawn was breaking across the river, and the Ganga was already dotted with people bathing and worshipping in the shallows. The city too was awakening to the monotonous chant of priests and the ringing of bells in hundreds of temples. A few fishing boats were out, and the customary shallow skiffs were intermittently lined up along the *ghats*, waiting on mourners scattered around the funeral pyres. Shakuntala sat on the steps, cradling Chuyia in her arms. Chuyia's pallor was frightening, and she appeared to be gravely ill. Shakuntala did not know what to do. Whom could she turn to for help?

A tall, ebony-skinned woman rose out of the water beneath them. As she came up the steps, slender and graceful, drops of water sparkling in her wavy hair, Shakuntala's heart stilled. But for her rich colour, it could have been Kalyani rising from the river. The woman glanced at Shakuntala and Chuyia. Wordlessly, she offered Shakuntala water from her pot. Shakuntala cupped her hands to receive the water, and gently washed Chuyia's face and cropped head and drank some. She wiped brown patches off Chuyia's neck and calves with her sari and realized with horror that they were congealed blood from cuts and wounds. The woman lightly ran down the steps and fetched more water. Chuyia hadn't even opened her eyes. "I will hold her while you bathe in the river," the woman offered, sitting down next to her.

"We are widows," Shakuntala said, looking squarely at the woman.

"I know," the woman said. "I am Gandhi's follower. I see things differently."

This woman did not care if their shadows fell on her and jinxed the rest of her day; she wasn't afraid to touch them. Shakuntala gratefully handed Chuyia over to her and went into the river to bathe.

Shortly after Shakuntala returned, somewhat restored from her bath, Chuyia opened her eyes. They were sunk in their sockets and muddy with broken capillaries. The skin around them was blotchy and bruised. Shakuntala dipped her sari in the pot of water the woman had left there and gently wiped Chuyia's face. Just for an instant, the child's gaze focused and a flicker of recognition sparked her eyes. Whispering, "Chuyia? I'm here. You're safe, you're with me," Shakuntala smiled. There was no answering smile in the vacant face.

As the sun began to climb in the sky and the drug began to wear off, Chuyia gradually revived. Shakuntala tried to stand her up, but her legs buckled. The child could barely sit, her back gave way and she fell forward. Chuyia wound her arms around Shakuntala's neck and lay supine against her, her body responding just enough so that she was easier to move, hold and carry.

Chapter Twenty-one

Rabindra was driving Narayan to the station. The top of the Model T Ford was down, and, as the wind rushed through his hair and stung his eyes, Narayan felt his mood lighten. He glanced at Rabindra, and his lips twitched in a reflexive smile; it must cost his loquacious friend to remain so quiet. He was grateful for the silence. He had hardly slept the past two nights, and his mind again wandered to the cataclysmic events that had brought his life to an abrupt halt with the death of his beloved Kalyani.

Narayan had kept well away from his father; he knew he couldn't bear to see the grizzled beard, the fleshy lips, the lascivious movement of the eyes beneath the hooded lids, without thinking of them peering at his Kalyani the way no man ever should. Narayan felt his hands squeeze the life out of his father as surely as he and his kind had killed his beloved. He shook his head to put a stop to the morbid direction his thoughts had again taken.

"Are you all right, old chap?" Rabindra asked.

"Yes," he said.

"You were a bit restless just then."

"Was I?" Narayan's tone was noncommittal.

Rabindra knew when to leave his friend alone. They drove in silence.

Narayan's mind wandered to his leave-taking of Sadhuram. As always, he would have preferred to pack his own bags, but not wanting to hurt the sentimental old retainer's feelings he had let Sadhuram help him pack. Sadhuram's eyes were moist as he folded Chhotay Babu's clothes with excruciating care and laid his shirts and *dhotis* in fluffy layers right on top. Narayan took his books from the shelf and piled the heaviest right on top of the clothes. The old servant didn't know if Chhotay Babu was teasing him, or if his grief had made him callous. Sadhuram just stood there, unabashedly leaking tears and brushing them away with the back of his hand. Then Narayan smiled—the first time he had done so since he lost Kalyani. He removed the books and folded the shrunken old man in his arms, holding him in a hug that lifted him clear off the floor.

"Chhotay Babu, you are too old to act this way," Sadhuram scolded, but Narayan knew nothing could have pleased him more. When Narayan removed Gandhi's portrait from the wall, Sadhuram gently wrested it from him and carefully wrapped it in a clean *dhoti*. It was the last thing he had packed, and it lay safe beneath the cushion of *dhotis* in his larger suitcase.

As if emerging from a dream, Narayan suddenly began to notice the lush landscape they were driving through. The tender green leaves on the branches of young trees arched over them, forming a shimmering canopy over their heads. The earth of the dirt road was red. The cloud of roseate dust they left in their wake and the banana groves and orchards on either side of them awakened him to the beauty of his surroundings.

"Feeling better?" Rabindra asked

Narayan nodded. "Sorry friend," he said. "I haven't been much company lately."

"It's understandable."

Rabindra changed gears to slow the car as they approached a small heard of goats crossing the road. Once they were past the herd, Rabindra turned to Narayan and said, "What are your plans?"

"I'll take the train and go wherever it goes: leave this place behind."

Rabindra nodded sympathetically.

"The absent are the dead—for they are cold," Narayan said under his breath, quoting Byron.

Rabindra glanced at his friend. Grief appeared to have marked his face with shadows, and he looked darker. "I'm sorry, Narayan," he said quietly, touched by his friend's pain.

PEOPLE WERE HASTILY CUTTING short their prayers and abandoning their ceremonial artifacts and water jars on the *ghat* steps as they rushed toward the alleys.

"Gandhi*ji* is here! Gandhi*ji* is here!" It was like an enchanted cry that everyone repeated in awed voices. Even those who had never heard of Gandhi were shouting "Gandhi! Gandhi!" and spreading the news of his imminent arrival all over the *ghats*. Shakuntala, carrying Chuyia, found herself swept up by the scrambling crowd and pulled into the teeming streets as if by an invisible thread. Instead of the names of gods and the holy river, it was Gandhi's name that echoed throughout the streets. Snatches of conversation filtered through Shakuntala's consciousness: "Gandhi*ji* is in here"..."At the railway station"..."On his way from Allahabad"..."Mahatma Gandhi is here"..."He's holding his prayer meeting"... "If you want his blessings, be there—"

Exhausted and dazed, Shakuntala was pushed along by the crowd as it wound its way through the last stretch of an alley and on toward the railway station. A group of men shouted, "Gandhi*ji* Zindabad!" and, picking up the cry, the crowd in unison roared, "Gandhi*ji* Zindabad!"

People pushed and shoved in their urgency to arrive at the station, but once they found a place to sit on the platform, they became calm and waited patiently for the Mahatma to speak. As Shakuntala picked her way through the crowd the people who were sitting on the platform floor shifted to make way for the widow. Chuyia's arms and legs were clamped tight around her, and the young girl adjusted her weight to help Shakuntala's movements. Suddenly, an arm reached out to pull Shakuntala down and, dumbfounded, she found herself sitting next to the woman who had risen from the river to offer them water. She looked even more radiant than Shakuntala remembered. She had a small red *tikka* on her forehead. She was not a widow, yet like all of Gandhi's followers she wore white. Smiling almost shyly, her teeth luminous in the oval of her chocolate face and her dark eyes lustrous, she ran her slender hand tenderly over Chuyia's head.

From where they sat, they could see Gandhi clearly. He sat cross-legged on a raised stage in front of a train carriage. The skinny, dark old man was naked except for the white *dhoti* covering his hips and thighs. His mustache was a white brush above his lips, and his head, bowed in meditation, was nearly bald. A child got up and placed a garland of lemony marigolds around Gandhi's neck. Gandhi raised his bowed head and ran his hand over the child's hair. He blessed a few other children who came to him. Shakuntala noticed his eyes; magnified by thick metal-rimmed glasses, they appeared to transmit an almost tangible aura of warmth and kindness, and an indefinable magnetism and power.

At some invisible signal the crowd grew silent, and in the wake of the expectant hush Gandhiji began to read out his speech. His quavering voice was high-pitched, yet his softly spoken words were distinct and clear. There was an endearing sweetness in the simple way he spoke that held his audience rapt. He put the sheet aside and, looking at the people around him, said:

"My dear brothers and sisters, for a long time, I believed that 'God is truth.' But today I know that 'Truth is God.' The pursuit of truth has been invaluable to me. I trust the same will be true for you as well."

There was a moment of complete silence after he finished speaking. And then, pandemonium. Amidst cheering and shouts of "Gandhiji Zindabad!" the shrill train whistle could be heard. Bent over his wooden staff, Gandhi stood up. His followers, in white homespun *khaddar* and white cloth caps, hustled him onto the dilapidated green train, which consisted of just two carriages. The British, cognizant of his power, had resignedly allotted the train to carry him and his followers across India to meet with a populace clamouring to see him.

Shakuntala had listened carefully to Gandhi's words. The closing sentence hummed in her head: "Truth is God." Not a person who easily gave her trust, she instinctively trusted this man. She had never heard the Deity spoken of this way, but then she was hearing things today she had never expected to hear. After Kalyani's suicide and the bestial horrors that had been perpetrated on the poor child in her arms, her convictions had been shaken; they could not be counted on to direct her life anymore.

A vague plan began to form in Shakuntala's head: Chuyia had to be saved from the assaults that would be inevitable if she were to go back to the *ashram*. All at once, she knew with a certainty she felt in her bones that Chuyia's only hope of rescue lay aboard Gandhi's train. She wanted to tell this to the woman sitting next to her, but the woman had disappeared. Her heart pounding, Shakuntala stood up and looked for her in the crowd. Chuyia must be handed over to someone and made to become a part of Gandhi's roving entourage. Gandhi's followers were kind and compassionate like him. They were filled with new ideas, new ways of viewing the world like Narayan was. They would not hold a child's widowed state or her past against her. They could take her far away from Rawalpur and the *ashram* and give her a new start in life.

Gandhi stood in the door, waving as the iron wheels of the train slowly creaked into motion and steam billowed out of its smokestack. Carrying Chuyia, Shakuntala pushed and shoved her way through the crowd to get closer to the moving train. Chuyia clung to her, confused. "Please let me through. Move aside," Shakuntala requested the people on the platform. And her voice carried an authority and purpose that made them do as she directed.

With a monumental effort, Shakuntala held the child aloft as she ran with the train, trying desperately to hand Chuyia over to any of Gandhi's followers who would reach out a hand.

"Brothers, please take her. Please take this child with you," she begged the *khaddar*-clad young people looking out the windows, standing at the open doors. "Listen to me... Why don't you listen? Why don't you understand? Sisters! Please take her with you! *Please* listen! This child is a widow."

But as the train, with an indifferent hiss of steam, moved past her, the people on it only looked shocked. "What are you doing?" a man scolded.

"Stay back, you'll get hurt!" shouted another.

"Are you insane?" someone cried.

As they refused to reach out their hands for Chuyia, Shakuntala's appeals became frantic. The steam-belching engine was slowly picking up speed. People on the platform tried to stop her. Afraid that the desperate woman might throw herself and the girl under the wheels of the train, a few women started to scream their alarm at the possibility.

The straining engine began to gather speed, and Shakuntala ran alongside faster. She was afraid she would stumble; her voice was becoming hoarse. Just then, a hand reached out from the train toward her and Chuyia.

Shakuntala looked up to see Narayan leaning precariously from the train, holding on with one hand,
extending the other to grasp Chuyia. "*Didi*!" he shouted.

Other people on the platform were running with her,
other hands reaching out to help her hold up the child.
Two men hung on to Narayan so that he could lean out
further. Suddenly, Narayan had an arm around the child
and he swept Chuyia up into his arms.

Shakuntala, still running alongside the train, out of
breath, pleaded, "Make sure she's in Gandhi*ji*'s care."

"Yes, *didi*," Narayan replied. And at that moment,
she saw the dark woman at a window a little farther down
the carriage. With a solemn look and reassuring gestures
of her expressive hands, the woman conveyed she understood: she would look out for Chuyia.

Shakuntala wanted to keep Chuyia in her sight as
long as possible, so she ran along the platform until the
platform came to an end. Exhausted, she sank down in a
squatting position and stared as the train carrying Chuyia
dissolved into the dark green trees in the distance.

Glossary

Agni Holy Fire

amma Bengali for "mother" or "mommy"

Arjuna an epic hero (of the Mahabharata)

ashram spiritual retreat centre

baba Bengali for "father" or "daddy"

bansari Indian reed flute

Bapu affectionate term for Gandhi

barsati a shelter from rain, usually on the roof

behen sister

betel leaf leaf wrapped around condiments and used as Indian chewing gum

Bhagvad Gita Hindu holy text

Bhagyalakshmi another name for the goddess of wealth and prosperity

Bhagwan God

bhaiya brother

bhajan song in praise of God

bindi red dot in centre of a woman's forehead symbolizing good luck or marriage

bitya daughter

Brahmin Hindu priest

Brahmanical rituals and traditions related to the Brahmin caste

bua auntie; used as a nickname for Patirajji in the novel

caste-mark marks on the forehead signifying the caste to which a Hindu belongs

chapati unleavened flatbread (like a tortilla)

charpoy the wooden frame of a cot that is interlaced with taut string to form a light bedstead

Chhotay Babu Young Master

Chuyia little mouse

daal lentil

Darbari a *raag*, known for its stately, meditative quality; it was played in the Mughal emperor's *darbars*, or courts

Dharma Ghat name of a specific ghat (an area on the river where people go to bathe in the holy river; also a location of funeral pyres)

Dharma Shastras text of religious laws

dholak **drums** small hand drums

dhoti cloth wrapped around the waist and tied between the legs

didi older sister

Diwali Festival of Lights

dom the man in charge of funeral pyres; belongs to the untouchable caste

Durga goddess of destruction

Durga Festival festival to celebrate the Goddess Durga

Gandhiji Zindabad "Long live Gandhiji"

ganga-jamuna game similar to hopscotch

ghat bathing area on the river; also location of platforms on which funeral pyres are lit

Gita Indian holy book

gopis Krishna's female consorts

gulab jamuns fried Indian sweets soaked in syrup

Hai Ram exclamation meaning "Oh God!"

Hajipur a city located in the state of Bihar, India

Haldi Uptan a ceremony in which turmeric is applied to beautify the bride

haram zadi daughter of a bastard

hijras eunuchs

hookah hubble-bubble, a smoking apparatus

howda a saddle on an elephant to accommodate people

Jai Shree Krishna salute to the god Krishna

japa incantation in which a god's name is repeated

jhola Bengali term for a large cloth pouch

ji a suffix added to a person's name in order to show respect for age or rank

Juthika Roy famous Indian religious songstress

kadamba flowering tree with large, white, ball-like flowers

Kalidas famous Indian poet

kanya daan giving away of daughter in marriage

karahi a wok-shaped pan used for frying

Karmi Ghat name of a particular ghat

katha **paste** a red betel-nut paste, which is applied to the fresh betel leaf for flavour

khaddar hand loom spun cotton

kheer a rice sweet

Krishna a god

kum-kum red paste used on ceremonial occasions

kurta a shirt

laddoo a sweet made of lentils

Lakshman brother of Ram

Lakshmi goddess of luck, wealth and prosperity (also
   called Bhagyalakshmi)

leechee a fruit

lingam black stone representing the god Shiva's phal-
   lus; symbolizes creative energy

Mahabharata book of holy Indian stories

Maha Shivratri main festival to celebrate the god Shiva

mandir Hindu temple

mangal-sutra a necklace worn by a married woman

Manusmriti Lord Manu's book of laws

Meghdoot cloud messenger

mishti-doi a sweet made out of yogurt

mithai Indian sweets

Mohandas Gandhi Gandhi's full name

moksha a liberation of the soul obtained through pure
   living

Nainital a hill resort in the south of India

nazar evil eye

Omkarnath Thakur famous Indian classical singer

oolu-oolu ululation

pallav the end of a sari which is thrown over the
   shoulder

pandal a platform on which weddings take place

pandit a Brahmin priest

pheras ceremonial circles made around wedding fires
   or funeral pyres

pradip oil lamp

pujari a Hindu priest

puris fried discs made out of flour

purohit priest

raag Indian classical tune

Radha name of a goddess

raj reign, or rule

Raja Ramohan Roy a social activist

Ram a name for God

Ramayana a holy Hindu text

Ram Naam Satya Hai religious chant meaning "Ram, your name is truth"

rasgullas cheesecake balls soaked in syrup

Rawalpur a fictitious city in the story

sadhu Hindu holy man

sari *palu* the end of the sari which lies over the shoulder

sarkar government

sati a ritual in which a Hindu widow cremates herself on her husband's funeral pyre

saubhagyavati fortunate

seths land owning gentry

Shashthi goddess of childbirth

Shiva a major Indian god

sindoor the red paste applied along the part of a married woman's hair

Sindoor Daan container for the *sindoor* (red paste); also the ceremony in which the red paste is applied to a bride for the first time

Sita Ram's wife, symbolizing purity

stri-dharma wifely duties

stri-svavahava a woman's lustful aspect

sumangali married woman

takth raised seating platform

thali a round metal platter

tikka a red mark on the forehead, worn by men and
women; also a piece of jewellery that decorates the
forehead

tulsi a plant considered holy by the Hindus (basil)

Tulsi Ghat name of a specific *ghat*

Upanishads Hindu holy texts

uptan turmeric paste considered auspicious

Vedas Hindu holy texts

Vriddha Hirata religious text

Acknowledgements

When Canadian publisher Anna Porter asked me if I would turn Deepa Mehta's film *Water* into a novel in three months—to time it with the film's release in the US—I was hesitant. I had never written within the confines of a structured story before, or the constraint of time. Deepa sent me the film script: it told a stunning story. She also sent me an early edit of her film, and it took my breath away. The songs by A.R. Rahman were enchanting. I agreed to give it a try.

I was able to complete the novel in time only because Deepa's film *Water* is so well-structured, and it is under-pinned by a complex density of feeling and information that helped me enrich and embellish the narrative. The excellent portrayal by all the actors was of enormous help with the characterizations. Sarala, who plays an eight-year-old child widow, was a joy to portray, as was the veteran actress Manorama in her role as the redoubtable ruler of the *ashram*. Seema Biswas plays a pivotal role in the film with passion and credibility. The gorgeous Lisa Ray, and the equally gorgeous John Abraham, will have audiences rooting for them with their poignant performances.

I would also like to acknowledge my debt to Heidi Boyd, who transcribed the film frame by frame and pried out details that facilitated the writing of the novel. I also thank Janie Yoon, my editor at Key Porter, for her valuable suggestions and encouragement, Tanaz Sunawala and Keya Mitra for their readiness to help, and Baku Karmani for her astute suggestions. I thank my husband, Noshir, for taking care of so many day-to-day matters while I was immersed in the writing.

I need to mention Delip Mehta, who recreated the burning *ghats* afresh in Sri Lanka, and made it possible for me to describe the landscape and fix the locale. He has added a dimension of beauty to the film, which in turn is brilliantly mirrored by the cinematographer Giles Nuttgens.

This is where I acknowledge my debt to Bibhutibhushan Bandopadhyay's magnificent novel *Pather Panchali*, which provided me with a feel for Chuyia's earlier life and surroundings. I also found *Widows in India,* edited by Martha Alter Chen, very helpful regarding the customs and traditions governing the treatment of widows in Indian society.

I undertook this project only because of my enormous respect for Deepa as a filmmaker and a friend. I previously worked with her on her 1999 film *Earth*, which was based on my novel, *Cracking India,* or *Ice-Candy-Man.* The film *Earth,* or *1947*, was the second in Deepa's trilogy, following the controversial *Fire*. *Water* completes the trilogy, and I'm honoured to be a small part of her dynamic vision.

About the Author

BAPSI SIDHWA is the internationally acclaimed, award-winning author of four novels: *An American Brat, Cracking India, The Bride* and *The Crow Eaters*. She is also the editor of the anthology *City of Sin and Splendour: Writings on Lahore* (2005). Her work has been published in ten countries and has been translated into several languages. Among her many honours, Sidhwa has received the Bunting Fellowship at Radcliffe/Harvard, the Lila Wallace Reader's Digest Writer's Award, the Sitara-i-Imtiaz, Pakistan's highest national honour in the arts, and the LiBeraturepreis in Germany. She has also been inducted into the Zoroastrian Hall of Fame. *Cracking India*, a *New York Times* Notable Book of the Year, was made into the film *Earth* by internationally acclaimed director Deepa Mehta. It was also listed as one of the best books in English published since 1950 by the Modern Library. Born in Karachi, Pakistan and brought up in Lahore, Pakistan, Sidhwa now lives in Houston, Texas.